"Puppies!" screamed Emily. "Come back!"

The puppies paid no attention—the thrill of the hunt was too strong to resist—and in a split second the four dogs had vanished into the throng of people crowding the midway.

"George!" Mrs. Newton ordered. "Go after them!"

Father and son took off. As they elbowed their way through the crowd, people turned and laughed good-naturedly. The four puppies had scuttled through only a few seconds earlier and it was obvious that Ted and George Newton were the anxious owners.

"Hey, mister," shouted one of the teenagers running one of the booths. "They went thataway."

He was pointing directly into the open mouth of the livestock auction tent. At just that moment the sound of a bull bellowing at the top of his lungs exploded out of the tent—followed by the distinct yapping of a quartet of Saint Bernard puppies . . .

Beethoven's Puppies

Family Vacation

A novel by
Robert Tine
**based on characters created by
Edmond Dantes and Amy Holden Jones**

BOULEVARD BOOKS, NEW YORK

BEETHOVEN'S PUPPIES: FAMILY VACATION

A novel by Robert Tine, based on the Universal theatrical motion pictures
entitled "Beethoven," written by Edmond Dantes and Amy Holden Jones, and
"Beethoven's 2nd," written by Len Blum. Based on characters created by
Edmond Dantes and Amy Holden Jones.

A Boulevard Book / published by arrangement with
MCA Publishing Rights, a Division of MCA, Inc.

PRINTING HISTORY
Boulevard edition / September 1996

The Putnam Berkley World Wide Web site address is
http://www.berkley.com

ISBN: 1-57297-168-1

BOULEVARD
Boulevard Books are published by The Berkley Publishing Group,
200 Madison Avenue, New York, New York 10016.
BOULEVARD and its logo are trademarks
belonging to Berkley Publishing Corporation.

PRINTED IN THE UNITED STATES OF AMERICA

10   9   8   7   6   5   4   3   2   1

Beethoven's Puppies

Family Vacation

1
...

"They're bad," said Mr. Newton. "And they're getting bigger. . . ."

"They're Beethoven's puppies!" wailed Emily.

"But, Emily," pleaded her father, "you have to see reason on this. You have to."

"But you promised!" the little girl sobbed. "You said that we could take the puppies on vacation with us!"

"Well, I didn't actually say—" But Mr. Newton never got the chance to finish his sentence.

"Yes you did!" Emily retorted sharply. "You absolutely said that we could take the puppies." She took a deep breath and her words came out in a rush. "You said it in the car coming back from Puppy Boot Camp and Mommy and Ryce and Ted and Beethoven and Missy heard you say it—so I have witnesses! You even crossed your heart!"

"But, honey," Mr. Newton implored, "you have to understand that it just isn't practical to take the four puppies on vacation with us. Where would we put them? There just isn't enough room."

Emily stared at her father with anger in her eyes, her mouth turned down like a sad clown. "You crossed your heart and promised. A promise is a promise," she announced. "Once you cross your heart like that and make a promise, you *have* to keep it. That's a rule. . . ."

Mr. Newton knew that he had gone down in his daughter's esteem, and while that was very bad, he also knew—and this was worse—that he was breaking her little heart.

"A promise is a promise," Emily repeated. "I can't believe you would break a promise, Daddy."

Mr. Newton shrugged helplessly and looked to his wife, Alice. "Honey, could you help me out here? Could you explain to Emily just how impractical it would be to bring the puppies on vacation with us?"

Mrs. Newton raised her eyebrows. "I don't know, George. A promise *is* a promise. . . ."

George Newton sighed heavily. He knew exactly what his wife was thinking. A month or two before this day, when it looked as if Beethoven and Missy's puppies had been lost forever, Mr. Newton had

2

attempted to cheer up his family by announcing that he had a wonderful idea for the Newtons' summer vacation.

They had been in the van, driving away from Colonel Happer's Puppy Boot Camp. The four puppies—Moe, Tchaikovsky, Dolly, and Chubby— had escaped from obedience school and were lost somewhere up in the mountains, deep in the dark forests that surrounded the Puppy Boot Camp. All three of the Newton children were profoundly depressed at the thought that they might never see the puppies again.

"You know," Mr. Newton had said, "vacation time is coming up and I was thinking of renting a boat. You know, rent a big cabin cruiser and go sailing for a couple of weeks."

Mrs. Newton had looked at her husband as if he had suddenly and without warning lost his mind.

"You were thinking of doing what?" she had asked. She knew that her husband did not know the first thing about boats.

But Mr. Newton had ignored his wife's concerns. "Don't you think that's a good idea? Kids, what do you think?" Mr. Newton had glanced in the rear-view mirror, hoping he would see three beaming faces, but they were still very concerned with the puppies and they looked only mildly curious about their father's vacation plans for the family.

Emily had broken the silence. "If we go away on a boat," she asked, "can we take the puppies with us?"

Now, Mr. Newton did not know much about boats, but he did know that there was no place less appropriate than a boat for two big dogs and four growing and rambunctious puppies. But right then it looked as if the puppies were gone for good. Emily looked so sad that he would have agreed to anything. . . .

He had said it rashly, without really thinking it through. "If the puppies come back, we'll take them with us."

The change in Emily had been immediate. "Really?" she asked. "You really mean it, Daddy?"

"Absolutely!" George Newton had said forcefully.

"Promise, Daddy?"

"I promise."

"Cross your heart?"

Solemnly, Mr. Newton had crossed his heart. "Cross my heart . . ."

Only Mrs. Newton had been worried about such a rash promise. "Don't go making promises you can't keep. Emily is like an elephant. She never forgets a thing. And she won't forget this, believe me. . . ."

"I tried to warn you, George," said Mrs. Newton. "I told you Emily would remember—and you *did* cross your heart."

"But you can't take dogs on a boat!" Mr. Newton protested. "They would only be in the way!"

"I'm not convinced that this boat idea is such a great one anyway, George," said Mrs. Newton. "You're not a sailor. You don't know anything about boats. And you know, I don't know anything about them either. So let's just forget the boat and go someplace nice. Like to the beach. We could rent a cottage on the shore and there would be plenty of room for the dogs. You will have fulfilled your promise and everyone will be happy." Alice Newton smiled brightly at her husband. "See, problem solved."

"Er . . ." said Mr. Newton, looking a little sheepish. He didn't meet his wife's gaze and she knew that meant that things weren't quite as simple as they seemed.

"Er?" Mrs. Newton asked. "Er? What's the 'er' for, George?"

"Er . . . nothing."

"George," said Mrs. Newton sternly. "Give me all the bad news now. I don't want to find out later that you've been keeping something from me. I don't want any surprises when it's too late to do anything about them."

"Well," said Mr. Newton reluctantly, "it might already be too late. In fact, I know it's too late."

"What is?" said Mrs. Newton. "Or do I even want to know?" She sighed heavily. "I don't want to know, but I suppose I *have* to know, don't I?"

"Well . . . it was supposed to be a surprise," said Mr. Newton. "But I suppose I could tell you now. . . ."

"George," said Mrs. Newton bluntly. "Once and for all, let's get this straight: I don't like surprises—unless you decide to surprise me with a piece of jewelry. Okay? Understand? Jewelry good. Everything else bad. Got it?"

"I understand," said Mr. Newton, nodding.

"Okay. Tell me."

"Well . . . I thought renting a boat was such a good idea, I put down a deposit on it already."

Mrs. Newton's eyes narrowed. "You what?"

"I said, I put a deposit down on it already."

"Well, get it back."

"I can't."

"Why not?"

"It's nonrefundable."

"Sheesh," said Mrs. Newton, burying her head in her hands. "How come I wasn't expecting you to say that?"

"Wait until you see the boat," said Mr. Newton enthusiastically. "She's really a beauty. Forty-two feet. Sleeps six. Full kitchen and main stateroom. Twin diesel engines. She cruises at eighteen knots—"

"Dad?" asked Ted. "What's a knot?"

"It's how you measure speed on water, son," said Mr. Newton, feeling very commanding and nautical.

6

"Yeah," said Ted. "But how fast is that?"

"Yes, Commodore," said Alice Newton. "Why don't you enlighten this family of landlubbers?"

"It's a . . . uh . . ." Mr. Newton cleared his throat. "Right. A knot is a nautical mile. Understand?"

Mrs. Newton and all three of her children answered simultaneously. "No," they said in unison.

"I'll try and explain it so you can understand it," said Mr. Newton, looking frustrated and annoyed. "The amount of time a ship takes to travel a nautical mile is known as a knot. Got it now?"

"But how fast is that?" asked Ryce.

"A knot," insisted Mr. Newton. "That's what a knot is."

"But how fast?" Ted insisted. "Translate it into miles per hour."

"Right, George," Mrs. Newton agreed. "If you tell me we're going a hundred knots, I won't know if that's fast or not."

"No boat can go a hundred knots," said Mr. Newton.

"See, I wouldn't know that."

"How fast can a car go in knots?" asked Emily.

"A car can't go in knots," said her father.

"Why not?"

"It . . . it just can't. . . ."

The Newtons stared at George and he shifted uncomfortably under their gaze. "What?" he asked. "What is it?"

"The truth of it is," said Mrs. Newton evenly, "you

7

don't know what you're talking about, do you? You just have this mental image of yourself up on the bridge of a boat with a captain's cap on your head steering the boat with a great big silver wheel, don't you?"

That very picture had popped into Mr. Newton's head, but he wouldn't admit it—at least, not in front of his children.

George Newton looked pained, as if offended by the ingratitude of his family. "It's not that. . . . I just thought it might be fun. And anything I don't know, I'll learn. Before you're allowed to take a boat out, someone from the boatyard sails with you and shows you what's what."

"George," said Mrs. Newton seriously, "are you sure you want to do this? Are you sure you're up to it?"

Mr. Newton nodded vigorously. "I want to do it," he said. "And I'm more than up to it. Besides, even if I wasn't—what about the deposit? We could never get it back and I'm not throwing money away like that."

"How much deposit did you put down?"

"Three thousand five hundred dollars," said Mr. Newton. He whispered the words, as if lowering his voice would lower the amount of money he had spent.

Mrs. Newton yelped. "Three thousand five hundred! You're absolutely right. We are not going to let that much money go to waste!"

"Good," said George Newton. "Then it's settled.

8

We're going on a boat trip. I'm glad we got that out of the way."

"But what about the puppies?" said Emily.

"Tell them to pack their bags," said Mrs. Newton. "They're about to become sea dogs!"

2
•••

Mr. Newton did manage to wring one concession out of Emily. She agreed that Beethoven and Missy would stay behind and only the puppies would go on the family's boating vacation. It was not easy to get the little girl to yield, though, because, as she said over and over and over again, a promise is a promise.

When her father suggested this course of action to her, the little girl looked very doubtful.

"Leave Beethoven and Missy behind?" she said. "That's not a very good idea, Daddy. They'll miss the puppies and the puppies will miss them."

"I know that, honey, but we just can't fit six dogs

on the boat. It cannot be done. There just isn't room."

"We'll find the room," said Emily earnestly. "They could sleep in my bed if they wanted to. They do when we're home here."

"Emily, try to understand. . . . We're talking about a boat. It's small. The rooms are small. The beds are small. One of the big dogs alone wouldn't fit in your bed—never mind two big dogs and little you."

Emily looked very sad. "But it seems so unfair. Why shouldn't Missy and Beethoven go on vacation like the rest of the family? They need a rest, too, you know. They work hard being dogs all year round."

Mr. Newton thought of all the things that had been chewed, scratched, buried, or otherwise destroyed in the last year by Beethoven and his brood. He nodded sadly. "I know exactly what you mean."

"Then they *have* to come, you see?"

"Well, you might find this hard to understand, Emily, but sometimes mommies and daddies like to have a little time away from their children. It doesn't mean they don't love them, you understand, but they just want some rest. . . ."

"But you and Mommy never take any time off from me and Ted and Ryce," said Emily thoughtfully. "At least I can't remember you doing that."

Suddenly a wonderful image popped into Mr. Newton's mind. There he was at the helm of the sleek white boat they had rented, the vessel cruising slowly through a calm sea under a brilliant blue sky. *And there was no one else on the boat except for his wife Alice!*

Emily noticed that a very odd, rather dreamy look had come over her father's face. His eyes seemed misty and his eyelids were half-closed, as if he was looking at something miles and miles away.

"Daddy?"

"Hmmmmmm?" said Mr. Newton.

"Daddy!" Emily snapped.

"Huh? What?" Mr. Newton's head jerked as if he had just been woken up from a deep sleep.

"I don't think you were paying attention to me," said Emily haughtily.

"Sorry, dear . . ." said Mr. Newton. "Where was I? What was it I was talking about again?"

"You weren't talking," said Emily. "I was."

"Oh yes?"

"You told me that some people like to go on vacation without their kids." Emily still looked puzzled by that odd notion.

"Oh yes," said Mr. Newton, straightening himself up, as if waking up from a nap. "Some people go on vacation without either their children *or* their dogs. Emily—I'm sorry. We just cannot take Missy and Beethoven with us."

"But who will take care of them?" Emily cried.

"I've already spoken to Mr. Fletcher. He says he'd be glad to look after them. And you know that he and Beethoven are old friends," said Mr. Newton.

"And remember, Mr. Fletcher is all alone in the world. I think he'd like a little company."

Mr. Fletcher was an elderly widower and the Newtons' next-door neighbor.

"Is he very lonely?" asked Emily.

"I think so," said Mr. Newton.

The thought of a lonely old man all alone in his house seemed to melt Emily's heart. "Then I guess they should stay home and help Mr. Fletcher," she said. "Beethoven and Missy know that would be the right thing to do. Right, Daddy?"

"Absolutely," her father said, nodding vigorously. He didn't say what he was really thinking: *I wonder if Mr. Fletcher knows what he's gotten himself into. . . .*

3
•••

There were a lot of details to be attended to before the Newton family set out on vacation. Mrs. Newton had to put all the clothes and luggage in order, while Mr. Newton went to a boating supply store and bought a whole bunch of maps and, secretly, a white captain's hat liberally embellished with gold braid.

As things became busier and more hectic and as the pile of bags and equipment needed on the voyage grew bigger and bigger, Mrs. Newton began to regret that she had permitted her husband to go ahead with the plans for such a complicated vacation. But it was too late to change anything now. . . .

Unbeknownst to Mrs. Newton, her husband was having the very same reaction. The plans were becoming more and more elaborate with each passing day. The boat they had hired was moored in a little town on Lake Michigan called Harbor Springs, and the process of moving two adults, three children, and four puppies from the Newtons' home town to the northern part of the Michigan peninsula was nothing less than daunting.

Mr. and Mrs. Newton decided that the family would fly to Detroit, rent a car there, and drive the two hundred and seventy miles to Harbor Springs. It fell to Mrs. Newton to book the flight. The first thing she discovered was that the puppies would not travel free, but had to have tickets at the cost of forty-five dollars each. In addition, the Newtons had to buy four puppy transporter cages, and they cost fifty dollars each!

Mr. Newton grumbled about the cost and made one last attempt to talk Emily out of taking the pups along. Needless to say, the little girl did not budge an inch! But she did not much like the idea of putting the puppies in cages and sending them to Detroit in the cargo hold of the airplane either.

"Daddy!" she exclaimed. "The puppies will be scared to death!"

"Well, Emily," said George Newton, "if you insist on taking them, then that's the way they have to travel."

"But it's cruel!"

"They'll be perfectly safe," said Mrs. Newton soothingly. "There's nothing to worry about, honey."

"You can't buy them seats like us?" asked Emily.

"No, dear," said Mrs. Newton.

"The airlines won't allow it," said Mr. Newton.

Emily was old enough to know that she could bend her parents to her will, but there was nothing she could do against a great big airline. "Okay . . . I guess they'll have to travel in the cages. . . ."

Beethoven and Missy knew that something out of the ordinary was definitely going on in the Newton household. All the hustle and bustle, the lists and piles of luggage suggested that the family was going away. Not only that, but Mr. Fletcher seemed to be spending more and more time at the house talking to Mrs. Newton about feeding schedules, the phone numbers of the pet supply store, and the veterinarian. Plainly, then, the busy doings around the house had something to do with them.

The puppies—Tchaikovsky, Moe, Dolly, and Chubby—had no idea that anything extraordinary was going on. They continued to live their lives as they always had—they played, they ate, they slept, and somehow managed to cause trouble no matter what they were doing! They clambered up and down the piles of luggage and burrowed into bags, undoing in a few minutes work that had taken a day to complete.

17

The day that Mr. Newton brought home the puppy carriers and left them in the hall, the four little dogs examined them, sniffing and pawing the containers with great curiosity. It was Moe, the smartest and most daring of the puppies, who first crawled inside one of the boxes. He turned around a couple of times then flopped down and snuggled against the smooth plastic sides.

"This is really cool," said Moe. "Now we each have our own little house. This was real nice of Mr. Newton, don't you think?"

Dolly, the *least* daring of the puppies, looked very suspicious. "Uh-uh," she said, her voice full of doubt. "There's no way I'm getting in one of those things."

"There's nothing to worry about," said Moe. "Look. See? I'm fine in here, aren't I?"

"But for how long?" said Chubby cagily.

"What do you mean?" asked Moe, a look of puzzlement on his furry little face.

"I'm surprised at you," said Dolly. "You're usually the smart one, Moe. Can't you see that they could pick you up in one of those things and carry you around? Me, I like to sleep on firm foundations!"

"Oh, come on," said Moe. "Why on earth would the Newtons want to carry us around? It's never going to happen. . . ."

"That's everything." Mrs. Newton sighed.

"Good." Mr. Newton slammed the hatchback door of the family minivan. All of the Newtons' luggage, equipment, and puppies were crammed into the van. All four of the puppies, each one loaded in a doggy carrier, stared out through the rear window. They looked sort of stunned.

"Why would the Newtons want to carry us around?" said Tchaikovsky sarcastically. "It's never going to happen!"

"Okay, okay," growled Moe. "So I was wrong. It's not like you're always right, you know."

Dolly was in no mood for sarcasm. "What's going on?" she mewled sadly. "Why have they locked us up like this? I don't like it at all."

"And what about Mom and Dad?" Chubby yelped. The four little dogs pressed their noses through the cage bars and peered at Beethoven and Missy. They were outside the van, standing in the driveway with Mr. Fletcher. Ryce and Ted had already said their good-byes to Beethoven and Missy. Now it was their little sister's turn. Emily had her arms thrown around both of the dogs' shaggy necks.

"Don't worry," Emily whispered to Beethoven and Missy. "We're going to take real good care of your babies. They'll have fun with us and you two can stay here and help Mr. Fletcher. You take care of him, okay?"

In reply, Beethoven's thick pink tongue licked her face like a paintbrush. Missy whimpered slightly—she hated being separated from her pups!

"Emily," Mrs. Newton called. "We have to get

19

going." Ryce, Ted, and Mr. Newton were already in the van.

The little girl gave the two dogs a final loving hug and then very reluctantly stood up. Mr. Fletcher patted her on the head.

"Now, you have yourself a good time, little lady," he said. "Don't worry about your two dogs here. They're going to be fine."

Emily nodded solemnly. "I know, Mr. Fletcher. They promised me they would take good care of you."

"Take care of me!" The old man laughed loudly. "Why, that's a good one. A *real* good one."

Mr. Fletcher was still laughing as the van rolled down the driveway.

"Well," said Mr. Newton. "Our vacation has officially begun. So how does everyone feel?"

"Great!" said Ted.

"Me, too!" said Ryce.

Mrs. Newton smiled and looked over her shoulder at her three children strapped into the backseat. "Emily? What about you?"

"I miss Beethoven and Missy," she said sadly.

"But we've only gone ten feet!" exclaimed Mr. Newton.

"You'll feel better, Emily," said Mrs. Newton.

From the back of the van came a howl from Dolly. "I won't," she wailed. "I feel miserable!"

4
•••

But the puppies' misfortune was only just beginning. When the van stopped at the airport, they
had a quick glimpse of the Newton family before
two skycaps grabbed their portable kennels and
shoved them through a heavy plastic curtain. One
after another, the four carriers thumped onto a
conveyor belt and carried the little dogs deep into
the bowels of the airport.

The four puppies lost sight of one another in the
dark and noisy interior of the airport. They all
started yelping at once, desperate to hear the
sound of each other's voice.

"What is happening to us!" Dolly howled. "What's going on?"

"Help!" yelped Chubby.

"Don't leave me!" cried Tchaikovsky.

"Everyone stay calm!" Moe shouted.

The four little boxes trundled through the airport, bumping along the conveyor belt with piles of suitcases and cardboard boxes. Suddenly the carriers tumbled onto a wagon that was hooked up to a tractor. As soon as the wagon was full of luggage, the driver turned on the engine and the little luggage train pulled out of the building and into the bright sunlight again.

The puppies felt a little better to be out in the light again, but their worries were far from over. The tractor hauled the carts across the huge expanse of concrete in front of the main airport building. The puppies stared bug-eyed at the things they saw as they were whisked along. There were huge airplanes, their jet engines screaming as they slowly taxied out to the runways. The luggage wagon raced by giant pieces of machinery that were loading meals into airplane galleys or massive red tanker trucks pumping hundreds and hundreds of gallons of aviation fuel into the wing tanks of the aircraft. The noise from all the machines and from the jet engines of the aircraft was deafening and frightening.

Of course, the puppies had no idea what all this meant. They just knew they didn't like it one bit! The luggage wagon came to a halt next to an airplane and men got busy taking the bags off the truck and slinging them into a giant hold in the belly of the aircraft.

The puppies gawked up at the tremendous airplane. "Are we going to get into . . . that thing?" said Moe, awestruck.

"I hope not," said Dolly in a very small voice filled with fear.

"Hey, look," said one of the luggage handlers. "Puppies."

"Yeah, great," said one of them without enthusiasm. He picked up Moe's cage and placed it in the cargo hold.

"Hey!" said Moe. "Wait!"

Next it was Chubby. "Noooo!" the little dog wailed.

Dolly yelped as she, too, was loaded into the airplane.

One of the men put his face up close to Tchaikovsky's cage and poked through the bars with his fingers.

"Hiya, boy," he said. "Gonna go on an airplane ride?"

Tchaikovsky did his best to lick the man's hand, whimpering as he did so. "Listen, mister," said Tchaikovsky quickly, "I don't want to go on an airplane ride. I have to get out of here in a hurry. Understand?"

"Aww," said the baggage loader. "Ain't that cute. He's a friendly little guy." With that, he picked up the cage and slid it into place next to Tchaikovsky's brothers and sisters.

23

"Okay," said one of the baggage handlers. "That's it."

The large cargo door swung closed and shut with a loud bang and a sharp hiss. All was darkness. The puppies were so scared they could barely speak. Finally Moe found his voice.

"I don't like this one little bit. . . ." he began.

"Well, I hope things don't get any worse," said Tchaikovsky glumly.

"Worse!" exclaimed Dolly. "How could things get any worse than this?"

"Impossible," insisted Chubby.

In that very moment things got worse. In the cold darkness a terrible noise invaded the room as the engines revved higher and the room began to move. . . .

Directly above the puppies, up in the passenger compartment, the Newtons were buckled into their seats, relaxing during the flight. All of them were relaxing, that is, except Emily.

"Mommy . . ."

"Yes, honey?"

"The puppies are on this plane, aren't they?"

"Of course . . . You saw the skycaps take their carriers."

"Well, can I go and see them?"

"I'm afraid not, dear."

"Why not?"

"Well, the puppies are in a special place where

24

puppies are supposed to fly, honey. Don't worry about them."

"But why can't I visit them?"

"Because the pilot wouldn't like it."

"Why not?"

Mrs. Newton had long ago learned that there was no way that Emily would accept an answer like "because I say so." She had to think fast to come up with something that would satisfy the little girl's intense curiosity.

"Well, you would want to see the puppies if you could, wouldn't you?" Emily's mother asked.

The little girl nodded vigorously. "Of course I would."

"And I'll bet the pilot would, too, wouldn't he?"

"Naturally," said Emily. In Emily's world, no one would pass up the chance to play with the four puppies.

"Well, if he went to see them," said Mrs. Newton, "who would be flying the airplane then?"

Emily's eyes grew wide. "Wow, I never thought about that!"

"Besides," said Mrs. Newton. "You'll see them soon enough. We're about to land."

As the flight went on and it became plain that nothing bad was going to happen to them, the puppies had settled down somewhat. They didn't like the darkness or the cold, but they were beginning to believe that they would survive the flight.

"I wonder what this is all about," Moe wondered aloud.

"Who knows," said Dolly.

"Remember," said Tchaikovsky, "we are dealing with humans here."

"Right," said Chubby. "Who can tell what kind of mischief they can get into?"

"They never make the least bit of sense," said Dolly.

In the dark, all four puppies nodded. They never ceased to marvel at the wacky ways of humans.

"Well," said Moe philosophically, "the Newtons may be humans, but they're almost as good as dogs."

"That's right," agreed Tchaikovsky.

"So I think that no matter how nutty they get, we should trust them," said Moe. "They would never hurt us. And they would never let anything bad happen to us, would they?"

"Never!" said Dolly.

"Absolutely not!" exclaimed Chubby.

"No way!" insisted Tchaikovsky.

"Then what are we worrying about?"

"Moe's right," said Dolly. "I feel much better!"

5
...

The Newton family was lined up in the baggage-claim area when the carousel began to move. All of a sudden the plastic curtains at the end of the conveyor belt swept open and a long train of bags started down the runway. As Mr. and Mrs. Newton scurried around grabbing the family luggage from the conveyor belt, the three children had their eyes glued to the opening, waiting for their first glimpse of the puppies.

"Where are they?" said Emily impatiently.

"I hope they got on the flight," said Ted.

"Maybe the airline made a mistake and the

puppies got sent to Cleveland by mistake," said Ryce.

"NO!" exclaimed Emily excitedly. "There they are!"

The first puppy carrier emerged from behind the plastic curtain—it was Moe's—immediately followed by the other three. The instant they saw the Newton children, all four of the puppies began barking excitedly and scratching at the bars of the cage doors.

"It's them!" Dolly yapped deliriously. "We're saved!"

"Thank goodness!" yelped Tchaikovsky.

"I'm glad that's over!" exclaimed Chubby.

Emily couldn't contain her excitement. She pulled open the door of Moe's cage and hugged him tight.

"Oh Moe! I'm so happy to see you! How was your first airplane flight?"

"Whoa," said Moe. "It was intense!"

"Did you enjoy it?"

"Nope," said Moe truthfully.

"Come on, kids," ordered Mrs. Newton. "Let's get going now. Daddy has the van out in front!"

The van was on the road fifteen minutes later and heading north for Harbor Springs. The puppies collapsed in a heap in the back of the vehicle and fell asleep before the Newtons had left the airport.

"I wonder what's going on at home?" said Ryce.

"I'm sure that Missy and Beethoven are having a wonderful time," said Mrs. Newton.

Things were awfully quiet around the Newton home with both the children *and* the puppies out of the picture. Not only that, Mr. Fletcher never seemed to do anything besides walk to the grocery store in the morning and buy something for his lunch and dinner. He would also pick up the paper at a corner newstand and then go home and spend the rest of the day reading it. At six o'clock he would turn on the television, watch the news while he cooked dinner, eat his dinner, read the paper some more, and then go to bed.

Beethoven and Missy were bored to death. . . .

Chubby awoke in the rear of the van and looked out the window at the passing scenery. The countryside was pretty, but the little dog was aware that there was something not right, something very bothersome. . . . Then it came to her in a flash!

"I'm hungry," Chubby moaned. "Really, really, *really* hungry . . ."

Of course, none of the Newtons could speak dog, so they couldn't understand her plaintive wail. However, Chubby was in luck, because just about that time, a similar thought was popping into Ted's mind.

"I'm hungry," said Ted. "Really, really, *really* hungry . . ."

"Me, too," said Ryce.

"And I'll bet the puppies are hungry, too," said Emily. "Breakfast was hours and hours ago."

"You know," said Chubby dreamily, "I love that little girl."

"Well, it *is* almost lunchtime," said Mrs. Newton.

"Do you want to stop now?" her husband asked, giving the distinct impression that he did *not* want to stop. "We're making really good time, and if we stop now we won't be able to get on the boat tonight."

"Then we should definitely stop," said Mrs. Newton quickly. "I don't *want* to get on the boat at night."

"Aww, honey . . ." Mr. Newton had visions of sailing off into a setting sun in his boat.

"Sorry," Alice Newton replied. "That's not negotiable. We're not getting on some boat you don't know anything about and heading out to sea."

"Look," said Ryce suddenly, pointing to a billboard by the side of the road, reading it quickly as it flashed by.

"What?"

"That sign said that there's a county fair in the next town," she said. "I bet we could get something to eat there."

Now, it so happened that George Newton had a weakness for the food served at county fairs—and his older daughter knew it.

"Well . . ." said Mr. Newton as if struggling with his conscience and sense of duty. "Okay . . . We can stop here for a while—that is, if you really want to."

30

"Yes!" all three Newton children said in a chorus.
"Yay!" cheered the puppies. "Foooood!"

It was a beautiful, sunny summer day and the small fairgrounds were packed with people, mostly local folks, with a smattering of out-of-towners, tourists just passing through like the Newtons. The fair was a typical country gala, a dozen or so big tents pitched in a field by the side of the main road. There were stalls and sideshows and games of chance. On the far side of the field, the upper arc of a small Ferris wheel seemed to tower over the fairgrounds. Most of the stalls were run by boys and girls from the local clubs like the 4-H.

Because this was farm country, the largest tent was full of men in denim overalls crowded around the livestock rings watching the annual auction of various types of farm animals—mostly, pigs, cows, bulls, and horses.

The scent of the animals was carried on the wind and the four puppies' wet little noses twitched and wrinkled when they caught the enticing smell. Tchaikovsky, Chubby, Dolly, and Moe were dogs from the nice neat suburbs and they had never encountered the odor of cows and other livestock before—but they were still dogs. The smell was delicious and bewitching.

"Hey," said Dolly. "Do you smell that?"

"You bet!" said Tchaikovsky.

"I don't know what it is," said Moe. "But are any of you thinking what I'm thinking?"

"I think so," said Dolly.

"Let's go chase it!" cried Moe.

With a howl the four puppies took off, racing through the crowds, following their noses, closing in on the scent.

"Puppies!" screamed Emily. "Come back!"

The puppies paid no attention—the thrill of the hunt was too strong to resist—and in a split second the four dogs had vanished into the throng of the people crowding the midway.

"George!" Mrs. Newton ordered. "Go after them!"

"Oh, Lord!" shouted George Newton. "Come on, Ted!"

Father and son took off, running more or less in the direction that the puppies had gone. As they elbowed their way through the crowd, people turned and laughed good-naturedly. The four puppies had scuttled through only a few seconds earlier and it was obvious that Ted and George Newton were the anxious owners.

"Hey, mister," shouted one of the teenagers running one of the booths. "They went thataway."

He was pointing directly into the open mouth of the livestock auction tent. At just that moment the sound of a bull bellowing at the top of his lungs exploded out of the tent—followed by the distinct yapping of a quartet of Saint Bernard puppies.

"Uh-oh!" said Ted.

They ran to the opening of the tent and peered into the gloomy interior. Sure enough in the middle of the show ring were Chubby, Dolly, Tchaikovsky,

32

and Moe encircling a two-thousand-pound black bull. They were barking their little hearts out! The bull blundered left and right, not quite sure where to go—wherever the giant beast turned, there was a yapping puppy in his path.

Ted and George Newton stopped and gaped.

"Oh no!"

The farmers in the bleachers watched the excitement with some amusement while the auctioneer rapped his gavel and shouted, "Come on, people! C'mon! We got three hundred head of cattle to auction off here. We don't have time for this kind of nonsense!"

He glowered down from the podium and took a long hard look at Ted and his father. It was obvious in an instant that they were not farmers.

"You there!" the auctioneer yelled—and he could yell loud.

"Um . . . Yes, sir?" said George Newton. He could feel every eye in the tent on him.

"Those there your dogs?"

"Well . . . My children's dogs, actually."

"Close enough! Get them the Sam Hill outta here!"

The farmer closest to Mr. Newton tapped him on the shoulder. "You better be careful, mister. Hercules don't look like he's in the mood for playing around."

"Hercules?" said George Newton nervously. "That wouldn't be the auctioneer, would it?" Inside he was

33

thinking: *Please don't let it be the bull,* please *don't let it be the bull!*

The farmer laughed. "The auctioneer? Heck no. Hercules is the bull. Biggest, meanest bull in six counties."

Mr. Newton paled. "Here, puppiespuppiespuppies," he chirped. "Come on, puppiespuppiespuppies . . ."

All four of the puppies stood their ground, growling menacingly at the bull as if they were protecting the entire fair against this dangerous beast.

All of the farmers were laughing now, but not at the puppies. Now they were laughing at Mr. Newton. He could feel his face getting red and hot and he was half hoping that the ground would open and swallow him up there and then.

But no such luck.

"Hey, mister," the auctioneer bellowed. "Get on in there and get them puppies right now!"

"But the bull . . ." Hercules had horns that looked like swords and he was beginning to paw the ground, putting his head down as if he was just about on the verge of charging.

"Don't worry," said the farmer. "Just distract him." The man took a large red kerchief from around his neck and handed it to Mr. Newton. "Here, take this. That oughta do it."

"Do what?"

"Distract him."

"I'm no bullfighter," said George Newton.

The farmer shrugged. "Well, suit yourself, but

34

that bull's gonna charge sooner or later, and if one of them cute pups ends up on the business end of one of them there horns, it ain't gonna be pretty."

"You're a farmer!" Mr. Newton yelled. "*You* do it."

"I'm a pig farmer," the man replied. "If that was a mean old sow in there, I woulda done it already."

"Look, I don't have time to—"

Before George could say another word, he saw Emily racing straight into the ring. "Puppies!" she yelled.

Mr. Newton felt his stomach loop the loop. "Emily!" The next thing he knew he was running straight at the bull, waving the kerchief and hollering at the top of his lungs.

"*Yaaaaaaaaaaaaaaaaaaaaaaaa! Getawaybuuuuu-uuuuuuuuuuuuul!*" The bull's huge head swung around and his eyes blazed as he caught sight of the small piece of red cloth. Suddenly the bull seemed more enraged, and as he bellowed, foam and spittle burst from his lips.

Out of the corner of his eye, George could see Ted, Ryce, Emily, and Alice racing around the ring grabbing puppies and heading for safety. That meant he could leave! But before he could turn to run, the bull charged.

Mr. Newton's mouth dropped open and fear rooted him to the spot. Vaguely somewhere he could hear people shouting—"Run!" "Daddy!" "George!"—but *he could not move a muscle*!

It was just like in the cartoons. George Newton

stood absolutely still as the bull seemed to get bigger and bigger the closer it got.

And suddenly the bull was there, right on top of him. Something made George hold the red kerchief out to his side. At the last possible moment the bull seemed to lose interest in Mr. Newton and turned his murderous fury on the little patch of red. The ground seemed to shake as the bull thundered by.

"Olé!" someone in the stands shouted.

The bull had raced straight through the red cloth square, right past Mr. Newton, skidding to a halt in the sawdust twenty yards from where he had started. He turned around and snorted at his enemy; he had a look in his eye that suggested that he just might be planning on taking another run at Mr. Newton.

"Don't push your luck, mister," the auctioneer said to George. "Time to get out of there, now."

"Good idea!" George Newton took to his heels and ran as fast as he could, running straight at the wooden barrier that divided the show ring from the grandstand. He vaulted the rail like an Olympic high jumper!

As soon as he was safe on the other side, he slumped against the wooden wall and tried to calm his hammering heart. All of a sudden the entire tent burst into applause, all the farmers in there shouting and clapping and stamping their feet.

A couple of them pounded Mr. Newton on the back. "Well, mister, you might look like city folk, but you sure knew how to handle that big old ornery bull."

Another punched him vigorously in the arm. "If old Hercules had gotten you on those big horns of his, they woulda gone through you like a hot knife through a stick of butter!"

Mr. Newton managed to smile weakly. "Yes, well, I guess . . . uh. Well, I've always wanted to try my hand at bullfighting. . . ." Weak in the knees, he managed to make his way back to his family.

"Daddy!" exclaimed Ryce. "You were so brave!"

"George," said Alice Newton slyly. "I guess we never knew how much you loved the puppies! You risked your life out there with that bull."

Mr. Newton looked over to the show ring and looked at Hercules. A couple of farmers had gathered around the big animal and were trying to calm him down. Never had an animal looked so huge.

"I'm so proud of you, Daddy," said Emily. "And the puppies thank you, too."

Mr. Newton turned and glared at the four little dogs. "Puppies!" he growled.

6

• • •

It took a while for Mr. Newton to settle down, but Alice finally managed to calm him enough to get him to eat some lunch. They bought home-baked bread, some cheese, and farm-cured turkey and laid out the meal at one of the picnic tables scattered around the fairgrounds.

The puppies were happy with some puppy food from the trunk of the Newtons' van—though all three kids slipped bits and pieces of their own lunch under the table as little treats.

"I don't ever want that to happen again," said Mr. Newton sternly. "It's too dangerous. There have to be some rules."

"Right," said Ryce, laughing. "Rule one—no more puppy bullfights!"

"That's not funny," said her father.

"Besides," Ted asked, "what are the chances of it happening again? I mean, when are we going to run into a bull again?"

"That's not funny either," George Newton snapped.

"Daddy's right," said Mrs. Newton. "There *do* have to be some rules about the puppies."

"Absolutely," said Mr. Newton. "They cannot be allowed to run loose. From now on, they must be on leashes at all times. Do you all understand me?"

Ryce, Ted, and Emily nodded solemnly.

"And before we set out on the boat, I want you to work out a schedule. Who's in charge of the puppies—I want them under control twenty-four hours a day. Understand?"

"Even when we're sleeping?" asked Emily.

"No. Of course not . . ."

"Then it won't be twenty-four hours a day, will it?" Emily insisted.

"Well, if the puppies wake up in the middle of the night and start wreaking havoc, you three will have to deal with it. Okay?"

"What's 'wreaking havoc'?" Emily asked Ted.

"Basically, it's anything the puppies do that freaks Dad out, Em," Ted whispered to his sister.

"Oh," she replied quietly. "You mean everything?"

Ted nodded vigorously. "Yup. That's exactly what I mean."

40

"So," Mr. Newton continued. "I want you three to work out a schedule of feeding times, walk times, all that sort of thing, okay?"

"Okay," said Ryce, speaking for all three, "you've got a deal."

The Newtons rolled into Harbor Springs at dusk, just as the sun was setting over the vast expanse of Lake Michigan. The little town was perched on a bluff over the lake, with houses stretching from the heights all the way down to the water.

Mr. Newton parked the van in a parking lot next to the principal town dock. Along the whole length of the dock were boats—sleek million-dollar yachts, small motorboats, sailboats, fishing boats, tiny training boats hardly bigger than a bathtub.

"I wonder which one of them is mine," said Mr. Newton. He had a faraway look in his eyes.

"Yours?" said Alice Newton, raising an eyebrow.

"I mean ours," George said, quickly correcting himself.

Now that they were finally at their destination, the entire Newton family was beginning to get excited about their boating vacation.

"I want that one," said Ted as he got out of the van. He pointed to a big motor sailer that must have been eighty feet long. "Dad, will our boat look like that one over there?"

"In your dreams," said Ryce.

"Not quite, Ted," his father replied. "Ours doesn't have masts and sails. Just an inboard engine."

41

"But will it be as big as that?"

"Uh, no . . . No, it won't be," said Mr. Newton. "But it will be big enough. . . . I wonder where Angstrom's is."

"Where what is?" asked Alice.

"Angstrom's Marine," he said. "They're the outfit that's renting us our boat."

"It's right over there!" said Ryce.

Sure enough, next to the town dock was a big building built right out over the lake. It was crowned by a weather-beaten sign reading ANGSTROM'S MARINE SUPPLY. BOATS SERVICED/SOLD/RENTED.

"That's it!" Mr. Newton almost ran to the main door of the building. His face fell when he discovered the door was locked. "Oh, no! They're closed already." He pressed his face against the glass like a child standing in front of a toy store.

"Well, you'll just have to come back in the morning," said Mrs. Newton. "I think you'll live through the night!"

"Don't bet on it," Mr. Newton replied with a laugh.

"This a real pretty town," said Ryce. "Let's look around."

"Good idea," said Mrs. Newton. "And, George, I give you permission to buy us all an ice-cream cone."

The puppies strained at their leashes as the Newtons walked up Front Street to Main Street. There were nice shops lining both sides of Main Street—antique stores, clothing stores, bookshops . . .

Ryce and Mrs. Newton exchanged a conspiratorial wink.

"I can't wait to come back here in the morning when the stores are open," said Mrs. Newton.

"Me neither," said Ryce.

"But we're shipping out in the morning. There won't be time," said George Newton.

"Shipping out?" said Alice. "George, you make it sound like you've signed us all into the navy."

"Well, you know what I mean. . . ."

"Look," said Emily. "There's an ice-cream place!"

"I want chocolate chocolate chip!" shouted Emily.

"Cookies and cream!" exclaimed Ted.

"Pecan peppermint crunch!" said Ryce.

"Coffee almond swirl!" said Mrs. Newton.

"Vanilla!" said Mr. Newton exuberantly.

"Figures," said Alice.

All the kids and Mrs. Newton exchanged a look— the one that says, *Dad, what a dork!*

A few minutes later they were all standing on the sidewalk happily licking their ice-cream cones. The puppies watched enviously and Emily could feel their longing eyes on her every time she took a lick. It made her feel really, really guilty.

"Okay, okay," she said finally. "You can all have one lick."

"Me first! Me first!" Chubby yelped.

Before Mrs. Newton could stop her daughter, Emily leaned down, proffering the mound of ice cream on the cone.

Chubby was beside herself with delight. Her long

pink tongue shot out of her mouth and curled around the ice cream, then *sluuuuuurp!* All of the ice cream disappeared into her mouth! Emily stood there stunned, holding an empty ice-cream cone in her hand.

"Ahhhh," said Chubby. "That really hit the spot!"
Ted was almost rolling on the ground, he was laughing so hard, and he was in danger of dropping his own ice-cream cone.

"Mommy!" said Emily.

"Well, you did say one lick. That was one lick!"

"One *big* lick!" said Ryce.

"I want another one," said Emily. "I want another ice-cream cone. . . ."

"Oh Emily," said Mr. Newton. "I know you'll just give it away to the puppies again."

"Well, I told them they could all have one lick and then Chubby went and hogged the whole thing!"

"Yeah!" growled Moe. "Chubby hogged the whole thing."

"Right," said Tchaikovsky. "You ate the whole thing."

"Didn't think about us, did you?" said Dolly angrily.

"I'm sorry," said Chubby regretfully. "But I have needs. . . ."

"Please, Daddy, please. I want another ice-cream cone!" There were tears in Emily's eyes now.

"Okay," said her father. "But you can't give any of it to the puppies. Understand me—oops!"
As he spoke the big ball of vanilla ice cream on

his cone rolled off like a boulder going down a mountainside. It landed with a splat in front of the delighted puppies.

Ted laughed so hard he was doubled over and—*splat!* He dropped his cone on the ground, too!

"Oops!" said Ted.

"More!" howled Dolly. "Yippeeee!"

Now Emily and Ryce were laughing like crazy! Mrs. Newton was smiling broadly and trying not to laugh at her son.

"Okay," she said. "Now all the puppies have had some ice cream. Happy now, Emily?"

The puppies chomped happily on the cones and licked up all the spilled ice cream until the sidewalk was spotlessly clean.

When it was all gone, Moe licked his chops with great contentment. "This is shaping up to be a great vacation!"

7
•••

The front desk clerk at the Harbor Inn was polite but firm.

"I'm sorry, Mr. Newton," he said. "We will honor your reservation for you and your family, but we do not permit dogs on the premises."

"Well," said Emily matter-of-factly, "I guess we're not staying here!"

Her father swung around and glared at her. "Please, Emily, let me handle this," he said sternly.

He turned back to the clerk. "Is there another hotel in town? One that does admit dogs?"

"I don't believe so, sir. I would also like to inform

you that the town of Harbor Springs does not permit dogs in restaurants."

Mr. Newton's shoulders slumped. "I knew it! I *knew* that bringing them was a bad idea."

"It certainly is unusual, sir," said the desk clerk.

Mr. Newton looked at the man sharply, wondering if he was making fun of him. He decided he was.

"Would you mind if the dogs stayed in the van?"

"They can stay anywhere you desire, sir," said the desk clerk. "*Except* in the Harbor Inn . . ."

"Emily," asked Mr. Newton through gritted teeth, "is that plan going to be all right with you?"

Emily nodded. "Sure, Daddy," she said sweetly. "Whatever you want."

Once all the bags were out of the van, the puppies expected that one of the Newtons—Emily more than likely—would let them out. But to their profound amazement, when the bags were out, they remained behind. Ryce, Ted, and Emily gathered around the car to break the bad news to the little dogs.

"Sorry, puppies," said Ryce ruefully. "But the hotel won't let you stay in the room."

"What!" said Moe. "They won't let us in! I don't believe it!"

"How can they do that to us! Is that legal?" yelped Tchaikovsky.

"And we're so cute!" said Dolly. "You can't argue with cute!"

"So," said Ted, "we've left the window open enough to give you air and we'll be back after dinner."

"Dinner! Did Ted say dinner?" said Chubby. "They're going to dinner without us, how could they do that to us!"

"I'm sorry," said Ryce. "But that's just the way it is. . . ."

The four puppies pressed their wet noses against the window of the van as they watched the Newtons walk away. . . .

"How do you like that?" said Moe.

"Not very much," replied Dolly. There was disgust in her voice.

"After all we've done for them today!" said Moe.

"Yeah," chimed in Chubby, grumbling unhappily. "We gave them all that fun and excitement with that bull back at the fair!"

"Yeah," said the other three puppies.

"And then we did all that work cleaning up the sidewalk after they dropped their dumb ice cream," griped Tchaikovsky. "They don't realize that we didn't *have* to do that, you know."

"Yeah," said the other three puppies. "That's right!"

Then a funny thing happened. . . . Chubby, who was leaning against the door, fell out of the van! Ted or Emily or Ryce—somebody—hadn't closed the door securely and now it swung open wide. For a moment or two all the puppies could do was gape at the open door and at Chubby as she struggled to her feet. Finally, the significance of this awesome event hit them.

"Wow!" said Moe. "We're free!"

"Yeah!" said Dolly.

"What do we do now?" asked Tchaikovsky.

"Let's go find the Newtons!"

"Right!" said Moe.

As fast as they could, they scurried down the street in search of their family. It was obvious that they weren't angry at the Newtons anymore!

The Newtons had chosen a restaurant on Main Street and they had been given a nice big table right in the window overlooking the street. They had ordered some of the specialities of the region— sautéed perch, duchess potatoes—as well as summer treats like corn on the cob and lush ripe red tomatoes.

The food arrived and they all began eating with great pleasure. Inevitably, talk turned to the boat.

"So where are we going to be going, Commodore?" asked Mrs. Newton. "Have you plotted a course yet?"

Mr. Newton had thought of little else in the past few weeks, studying the *Great Lakes Pilot* books carefully.

"Well, I thought we'd start off with a short trip, just to get settled on the boat. That's called a shakedown cruise."

"That's a very good idea," said Mrs. Newton.

"Then what, Dad?" asked Ted.

"Then I thought we might go to an island in the middle of the lake called Silver Birch Island," said Mr. Newton. "It's about a three-hour cruise away."

"How many knots is that?" asked Ryce mischievously.

"Very funny," said Mr. Newton. But he was ready for the question. He cleared his throat. "It just so happens I did a little research and read up. For your information, a knot is a unit of speed of approximately one-point-one-five statute miles. Furthermore, you should know that in nautical terms a knot is a unit of speed, not of distance. I hope that clears things up for you."

But his children and his wife just gaped at him.

"What did he say?" asked Ted.

"I don't know," said Emily. "Was it even in English?"

"I couldn't tell," said Ryce. "What do you think, Mom?"

"Well, I know for sure it was English. As for what it meant—" Mrs. Newton shrugged. "Well, that's anyone's guess."

George Newton looked exasperated. "It's really very simple. You see, you measure a statute mile on water in a different way than you measure a statute mile on land."

"What's a statue mile?" asked Emily.

"Statute," he corrected.

"Stachoo . . ." Emily repeated.

"No, no, no—stat-tewt."

Emily appeared to have lost interest in the entire question. "Whatever," she said with a dismissive shrug.

But Mr. Newton was determined that his family understand what a knot was. "Okay, listen up. A knot is a measure of—" Suddenly he stopped speaking and his jaw dropped.

The family stared at him for a minute. "Dear?" said Alice Newton. "Honey? George?"

"I think Dad has forgotten the answer to his own question," Ted whispered to Emily.

Then, with a trembling hand, Mr. Newton pointed toward the window of the restaurant. The Newtons looked in the direction he indicated.

The puppies had found them, and four little noses were currently being pressed against the glass as the dogs gazed at their beloved family.

"It's . . . it's not possible," Mr. Newton stammered. "How do they do these things? *Why* do they do these things?"

"They just want to be with us, Daddy," Emily explained. "It's just as simple as that."

Mr. Newton put his head down on the table. "Why me?" he moaned. "Why does this always happen to me?"

Outside the restaurant, the puppies looked at the Newtons, watching as Mr. Newton lowered his head.

"Look," said Moe. "He's so happy to see us, he's overwhelmed!"

"Well, what did you expect?" said Chubby. "We're as dear to him as his own children are!"

8
• • •

As they walked back to the hotel, the puppies running around wildly—the dogs had, thoughtlessly, neglected to bring their leashes with them when they escaped from the car—Mr. Newton was strangely quiet. That worried Mrs. Newton quite a bit because she was sure he was thinking of a way to send the puppies back home before they took delivery of their boat. She felt terribly torn. On one hand, Alice knew her husband was right—the events of their first day of vacation had proven that the puppies could be a nuisance and would become even greater ones in the cramped confines of the motorboat. However, she also knew that there was no easier way to make her family unhappy than sending the puppies away. Emily would brood about it for days and days, possibly for the entire vacation.

Mrs. Newton really dreaded the possibility that her husband was going to suggest getting rid of the puppies.

"You know," he began, after being silent for most of the walk back to the hotel, "I've been thinking . . ."

Alice steeled herself for what she knew was coming next. "Yes, dear," she said. "I knew you were. . . ."

"I think I have an idea that will solve one little problem," he said gravely. "I hope I'm not going to get too much opposition."

"What do you think, George?" she said sharply. She could not believe that even her husband could be so naive as to think that having come this far, he would encounter no opposition if he suggested sending the puppies back.

"Well, it all depends on the hotel," said George slowly. "I mean, if they find out, I'm not sure *what* we'd do."

Alice looked puzzled. "The hotel . . . ? What on earth are you talking about, George? What does the hotel have to do with anything?"

"Well, I know it sounds crazy," he said sheepishly, "but I think we should try and smuggle the pups into the hotel. After all, it's only one night, and if we left them in the car they might get out again. And I'm afraid of what might happen to them."

Mrs. Newton did a double take so huge it was

almost theatrical. It was as if her husband had suddenly started babbling in a foreign language.

"George, I'm amazed. You do care about the puppies after all!"

"It's more than that," he said quietly. "I really care most of all about keeping the family happy. . . ."

The flinty-eyed desk clerk who had checked the Newtons in but thrown the puppies out was still on duty behind the reception counter in the lobby of the Harbor Inn.

The Newtons strolled into the hotel, each wearing a big phony grin pasted on their faces. Mr. Newton carried a large suitcase.

"Good evening!" George Newton said with an extra-strength dose of cheerfulness.

The rest of the family followed his lead. "Good evening!" they all said in a chorus.

"Good evening," the desk clerk replied. He eyed the suitcase suspiciously. "I was under the impression that you had unloaded all your luggage already, Mr. Newton."

"Nope. Forgot one. Ha-ha."

"Ha-ha," echoed Mrs. Newton.

"And are all your doggies bedded down in the van?"

"Oh yes, yes," said Mr. Newton quickly. "All bedded down, snug as a bunch of bugs in a rug."

"Snug," said Ryce.

"Real snug," Ted added.

"I'm glad to hear that," said the clerk.

"Well, good night," said Mr. Newton.

"Good night," said all the other Newtons.

The family stepped into the elevator, and sighed with relief as the door closed.

"You think he bought it?" Ted asked.

"I hope so."

Suddenly the suitcase in Mr. Newton's hands began to wriggle and in a moment Moe's head popped out.

"Hi, guys!" he growled happily.

"Shhhhhh!" said the entire family.

The Newtons and their dogs tiptoed down the hall to their rooms and let themselves in. They had two rooms adjacent to each other with a connecting door between.

"Now," said Mr. Newton in a low whisper, "we have to keep the puppies very, very quiet. Do you all understand?"

Mrs. Newton and the children nodded dutifully.

"So," he continued, "let's all go to bed early and get up early so we can get up and get going."

"Good plan, Dad," said Ted.

"We'll get a good night's sleep and be bright-eyed and bushy-tailed in the morning."

Dolly awoke in the middle of the night and whimpered quietly. Moe, Chubby, and Tchaikovsky awoke immediately thereafter.

"Dolly," said Moe, "what's the matter?"

"I miss Mom and Dad," she said sadly.

By himself,
a puppy like Moe
can get into trouble...

Unless Beethoven is around to keep an eye on him.

Why thanks,
Mr. Newton!
Coffee sounds great!

Packing up the puppies for vacation is hard work…

But at least they don't
have any luggage!

Hey!
Where's Dolly,
Chubby, and Moe?

Oh! Here they are!

All the puppies were silent for a long moment as they thought about what their sister had said.

"You know," whimpered Tchaikovsky, "I hadn't thought about it until now, but I kinda miss them, too."

"Me, too," said Moe sadly.

Chubby snuffled loudly and then suddenly let rip with a long loud howl. "I want my mommy!"

Now there is nothing more infectious to a puppy than hearing another puppy howl. The instant Chubby started to howl, Dolly joined in, adding her own powerful voice to her sister's loud, long wailing cry.

"I miss my daddy!"

Tchaikovsky and Moe tried to hold out as long as they possibly could, but at the mention of Mommy and Daddy, it took only a few seconds before the entire hotel was ringing with the sounds of yowling puppies!

Mr. Newton came flying into the room at the same moment the children tumbled out of their beds.

"Be quiet!" Mr. Newton shouted.

Ryce, Ted, and Emily fell on the puppies, trying to smother their howls. "Please, puppies," Ryce whispered. "You have to be very quiet."

"Yeah," whispered Ted. "You have to be quiet or Dad is going to have a heart attack."

They all held their breath and listened intently, wondering if anyone had been awakened. The hotel was silent.

"I think we're okay," said Ted after a minute or two.

"Yeah," said Emily. "I think we got away with it."

"I hope so," said Mr. Newton. Wearily, he turned and retraced his steps to his bedroom.

The instant he got back into bed, however, there were three sharp knocks on the bedroom door.

"Uh-oh," whispered Alice Newton.

Mr. Newton groaned and rolled out of bed. When he opened the door he found the desk clerk standing there, his hands on his hips.

"Well, Mr. Newton," he said. "It seems we have a problem here. . . ."

9
•••

The next morning when Mr. Newton awoke, he knew that things were not as they were supposed to be. For one thing, he felt very, very cold, which is unusual if you usually wake up in a snug king-size bed. Then he realized that every bone and muscle in his body seemed to ache. *Then* he realized that he was covered in puppies; all four of the little dogs were sprawled on his chest sound asleep.

Then it all came back to him. . . .

The desk clerk had insisted that the dogs vacate the premises immediately and the Newton family had insisted that the dogs could not sleep in the car alone. None of the kids was allowed to sleep in the

61

car and Mrs. Newton would not—so it fell to George's lot to baby-sit the pups out in the car. Folding his six-foot-plus frame into the narrow backseat of the car had not been easy and it was made more difficult by the fact that the puppies kept on climbing on him. Finally, he banished the little dogs to the front seat, but the instant he fell asleep they crawled over the seat back and settled on him like furry dew.

The first thing Mr. Newton saw when he finally summoned up the courage to open his eyes was Chubby's shaggy butt.

"Get off me!" Mr. Newton said.

The sleeping puppies scarcely stirred. Moe opened one eye, yawned and stretched, then closed his eye again.

Mr. Newton's temper flared. "I SAID GET OFF ME!"

They were so startled by this sudden bellowing that all four of the puppies seemed to bolt straight up in the air! Then they all came down on Mr. Newton's chest and closed their eyes again.

"Hey," grumbled Dolly. "You want to keep it down there? Some canines are trying to get a little shut-eye here."

"Really," said Tchaikovsky.

"Show a little consideration, pal," said Moe.

Mr. Newton roared again and struggled to stand up, dumping all four of the puppies on the seat.

"Argh, oooh, oh," Mr. Newton moaned as he felt his muscles stretch and stretch and strain. He felt tired and terrible, far from bright-eyed and eager as he had hoped to be for his first day on the water.

He stumbled out of the car and stretched again, trying to make himself feel better. But nothing seemed to work—until he caught sight of the lake. In the golden morning light, it looked placid and calm, wisps of night mist still hanging here and there. The little lighthouse on Harbor Point was still winking on and off every five seconds. The whole scene was beautiful, and instantly he felt his bad mood lift.

Chubby pawed his ankle. "Hey, George!" she barked. "I'm hungry!"

"Get back in the car," Mr. Newton growled. He loaded the puppies back into the car then walked stiffly into the hotel. The desk clerk was already at his post looking perky and wide-awake.

"Good morning, Mr. Newton," he said impishly.

"Good morning."

"Sleep well?"

"Blissfully, thank you," said Mr. Newton. "Sleeping out in the open air, under God's own stars . . . well, there's just nothing like it."

"Glad to hear it," said the desk clerk.

As soon as Mr. Newton reached his room upstairs, he collapsed on the bed. "Up and at 'em," he moaned.

By ten-thirty that morning, Mr. Newton had had his nap (as well as a shave and a refreshing shower), the bags were packed, the dogs had been fed, and the family was ready for the great moment—to finally meet their boat.

Mr. Angstrom, the owner of the boatyard, was waiting to meet them when they got down to the dock.

"Pleased to meet you folks," he said. Then he caught sight of the dogs. "You know, I always say that every boat should have a dog. . . . But four of 'em? That's going a little far, isn't it?"

"Is there a problem?" said Mr. Newton, his heart sinking. It had never occurred to him to check to see if Mr. Angstrom permitted dogs on the boats he rented.

"Nope," said Mr. Angstrom genially. "I don't have a problem with it if you don't, Mr. Newton."

George Newton felt his spirits lift again. "No, no problem here," he said good-naturedly.

"Good," said Mr. Angstrom. "Let's go meet your boat."

Mr. Angstrom led them through the boatyard and out onto the Angstrom home dock.

"There she is," Mr. Angstrom said, pointing to a sleek white cabin cruiser moored on the dock. "She's called the *Day by Day*."

The whole family stopped and gazed at the beautiful boat. For Mr. Newton, the moment was even more thrilling than he'd thought it would be. And, to his great satisfaction, the sight of the boat seemed to excite his family as well.

"George," said Alice Newton, "this boat is gorgeous!"

"Coooool," said Ted.

"Wow," said Ryce, "it's really nice, Daddy."

"Where do the puppies sleep?" asked Emily.

"Let's go aboard," said Mr. Angstrom. He stepped off the dock and onto the boat, then turned and helped Mrs. Newton aboard.

The instant Mr. Newton came aboard he went to the cockpit and put his hands on the big shiny ship's wheel. "Hello, boat," he whispered.

"Okay," said Mr. Angstrom. "This is a forty-two-foot motor diesel yacht made by Tiara of Holland, Michigan. It's a sweet boat. Handles real well, and even at this size she's pretty easy to run. Now, Mr. Newton, are you an experienced sailor?"

"Well, uh," said Mr. Newton, "I know the basics and I've, uh, been on a boat before and—"

"And he has his own hat," put in Emily.

"Okay," said Mr. Angstrom. "The first thing you do when you come aboard is start the blowers." He pressed a button on the control panel and two powerful fans started. "That takes care of any fumes that may have built up. . . . Now, if you'll step up here to the cockpit . . ."

As Mr. Angstrom took George through the boat, Alice, the children, and the dogs wandered through the ship admiring the small, but comfortable main stateroom and the two sleeping cabins. There was a small but compact kitchen and a small dining nook.

"This is terrific, Mom," said Ryce.

"Yeah," agreed Ted. "For once Dad has really done something right."

"Come on," said Mrs. Newton. "Dad does a lot of things right."

"Yeah," Ryce admitted. "But you know what I mean. . . ."

"Yes, I do," said Mrs. Newton. "Unfortunately."

Up on the main deck, Mr. Newton and Mr. Angstrom had finished the control check and were ready to take the boat to sea.

"Let's get your crew together, Mr. Newton."

"Family on deck!"

The Newtons came up from below and assembled in the stern of the boat.

"Okay!" said Mr. Angstrom. "The boat is tied to the dock with three ropes—we call them lines. The one in the front is the bowline, the one in the stern is the stern line, the one in the middle of the boat is the—"

"Middle line," said Emily.

"Nope. It's called the spring line," said Mr. Angstrom. "Mrs. Newton, the last line off is the spring line. You should take that one. You, son"—he pointed to Ted—"you take the stern line. That one comes off first. And young lady," he said to Ryce, "you take the bowline."

"Ted," said Mr. Newton, "take off your line. Now you, Ryce . . ."

Mr. Angstrom started the engine, Mr. Newton took the wheel, Alice slipped her line, and the ship gracefully sailed out into the bay. . . .

10

###

The training session lasted for most of the day, until Mr. Angstrom was convinced that George had mastered the basics of seamanship. As they headed into port, Mr. Angstrom gave his last words of advice.

"Don't try to put her anyplace tight, you don't know enough about boats to dock her anyplace close. Don't fight the weather. If there's a blow coming, you stay put. Understand?"

"Yes, sir," said Mr. Newton.

"And don't try to cruise too far. A couple of hours at a stretch. Otherwise you'll get tired—and when you get tired, you get sloppy."

"Got it!"

Mr. Angstrom peered over the bow of the ship. "You see that open berth over there?" He pointed to an open spot at the Angstrom's Marine home dock.

"Yes," Mr. Newton replied.

"You can drop me off there."

Mr. Newton gulped and took the wheel. He was extremely aware of the curious eyes of his family watching him for signs of nervousness or ineptitude, but he was determined to show them that he knew what he was doing. He squared his shoulders and faced forward like an old salt, then slowly throttled back, slowing down the boat gradually until it was hardly moving in the water.

"That's it . . . steady now," said Mr. Angstrom.

The boat glided across the smooth water and came to rest alongside the dock with scarcely a jolt.

"Excellent!" said Mr. Angstrom. "You handled this boat as if you've been doing it all your life!"

There was a smattering of applause from the Newtons. "Yaaaay, Dad!" Ted shouted.

"George," said Alice Newton. "I am well and truly impressed."

Even the four puppies looked in awe of George Newton's newfound seafaring skills.

Mr. Angstrom stepped off the boat. "Okay," he said. "See you in a week. Be safe now."

Alice Newton joined her husband in the cockpit. "Okay, Commodore," she said. "Let's go sailing."

The *Day by Day* cruised across the bay, around Harbor Point, and out into Little Traverse Bay.

"Where are we going, Dad?" Ryce asked.

"I thought we'd go down to Sutton's Bay." He pointed to a spot on the map. "Right there . . ."

"How many knots away is that?" asked Ted.

"Don't start that," said Mr. Newton.

The puppies sat in the stern of the boat; none of them was quite able to figure out what was going on.

"It's like a car," said Moe. "It moves . . . but on water."

"Humans are just too weird," said Dolly.

"It's awfully noisy, too," said Tchaikovsky.

"I wonder where we're going?" asked Chubby.

"You never know with this crowd," Moe observed.

Chubby yawned and stretched. "I think I'll take a nap. Wake me up if they decide to serve a snack."

"Nap," said Dolly. "That's not a bad idea." She settled down next to Chubby, put her head on her paws, and closed her eyes.

"I'm going to go exploring," Moe announced. "I want to look around some more."

"Me, too," said Tchaikovsky.

"Come on!" said Moe, leading the way.

The two puppies scampered across the deck and down the stairs into the main cabin.

"It's like a house *and* a car on the water," said Moe, amazed at the luxury in miniature in the boat.

"Wild," said Tchaikovsky. He hopped up on the sofa and snuggled down in the cushions. "Mmmmmm," he said. "This is sooo soft. . . ."

"I don't want to take a nap," said Moe. "I want some excitement!" He scurried away, farther into the ship. He squeezed under a bed in the forward cabin and found a ventilation duct that opened into the dark interior of the boat.

The noise of the engines was much louder now. Consumed with curiosity, he forced himself through another small hole in the wall and wriggled into the tight space. Then he realized he was in trouble. . . . He was stuck!

Up on deck, no one noticed Moe's absence. The three other puppies were still lazing around the boat, Mr. Newton was still at the wheel, the kids and Mrs. Newton were on the forward deck gazing at the shore or up at the huge dome of blue sky.

Suddenly Dolly woke up and looked around. She could sense that there was something very, very wrong. "Where's Moe?" she asked. Chubby could feel Dolly's fears.

"What's the matter?"

"It's Moe. He's gone."

The two dogs got to their feet and scurried down the steps into the stateroom. Tchaikovsky was sprawled on the couch, snoozing happily.

"Tchaikovsky!" yapped Dolly. "Where's Moe?"

Tchaikovsky yawned and stretched. He had been in such a deep sleep that it took him a moment to remember where he was—and where Moe had said he was going.

"You know Moe," said Tchaikovsky. "He said he was going to explore this place."

"Where? Which way did he go?" asked Chubby insistently.

Tchaikovsky inclined his head toward the forward cabin. "He went that way. What's up anyway?"

"Do you ever have that funny feeling," said Dolly, "that feeling that something is not quite right?"

"Yeah," said Tchaikovsky.

"Well, I got it. About Moe."

"Uh-oh," said Tchaikovsky.

The three little dogs ran into the little cabin and stood absolutely still. "I'll bet he crawled under there," said Tchaikovsky, peering under the bed.

"That would be just like him," Dolly agreed.

"I'm going down there after him," said Tchaikovsky.

"Don't be ridiculous!" said Chubby. "You'll get stuck down there and then what'll we do?"

"Come down after me!" Tchaikovsky called back over his shoulder.

Moe had wriggled and wiggled, he writhed and squirmed, but all he seemed to do was wedge himself into the pipe even tighter.

"Oh boy," he muttered. "I am in trouble now." He knew there was only one thing for him to do. Moe filled his lungs with air and then let out the loudest howl he could manage. But it could hardly be heard over the noise of the twin diesel engines.

71

Moe felt his heart sink. This was *really* bad.

Then, from behind, he heard something. "Moe!" Tchaikovsky barked. "What are you doing down here?"

"Am I glad to see you!" Moe yelped happily. "I'm stuck! What are you doing down here?"

"I came looking for you. We were all worried about you."

"Thank goodness for that!" said Moe. "Now give me a good hard push in the butt and get me out of here!"

"I'd like to," said Tchaikovsky. "But I can't."

"Can't? Why not?"

Tchaikovsky sighed. "'Cause I'm stuck, too!"

11

•••

Chubby and Dolly waited impatiently for Tchai-kovsky to come back, but with a growing sense of dread.

"This is nuts!" said Dolly.

"What do we do?" Chubby asked anxiously.

"Well, I know one thing," said Dolly firmly. "I am not going down there to get them."

"Then I guess I'll have to do it," said Chubby.

"What!" yelped Dolly. "You're going to go and leave me all alone! You can't do that!"

But Chubby was already wriggling under the bed, her rump sticking out. "You know, Dolly," said

73

Chubby, her voice muffled, "you better go get the Newtons right away."

"Why?" Dolly wanted to know.

"'Cause *I'm* stuck!"

That was all Dolly needed to hear. She turned around and raced for the stairs up to the main deck, her little legs slipping and sliding on the polished teak floors. She was yapping at the top of her voice.

"Help! Help! Help!" she bowwowed. "You have to come quick and help Moe, Chubby, and Tchaikovsky!"

The first person she encountered was Mr. Newton. He was still standing in the cockpit of the boat with his captain's hat on his head, daydreaming about owning a boat of his own and sailing around the world—without dogs. He was so deep in his daydream that it took him a moment to notice the small dog jumping halfway up his leg and yapping insistently.

Now, if there was one thing Dolly hated it was being ignored. "Hey! Hey! Hey!" she yelped.

Then, still not getting his attention, she jumped and sank her claws into his legs, like a cat climbing a tree.

Now *that* finally got Mr. Newton's attention!

"Yeeeow!" he howled, jouncing his leg wildly, trying to shake off the tenacious puppy. "Get off of me!"

George's loud bellows brought his family running

from the foredeck of the boat. But when they arrived, they could only stand and gape at the sight of their father/husband desperately trying to control the boat with one hand while trying to peel the puppy off his pants with the other.

"Help!" roared Mr. Newton.

Emily jumped forward and grabbed at Dolly. "What are you doing to Daddy?"

"Yap! Yap! Yap!" Dolly barked. In other words, "Help! Help! Help!"

Now that Dolly was under control—that is to say, no longer attached to his leg—Mr. Newton shook his head. "Could someone tell me what on earth *that* was all about?"

"Maybe Dolly wants to drive the boat," said Emily.

"Maybe she's seasick," suggested Ted.

"Maybe it's sunstroke," said Ryce.

"Maybe these dogs have gone and lost their minds once and for all," Mr. Newton concluded sourly.

It was Mrs. Newton who was watching Dolly the most closely, though. Dolly was darting toward the gangway stairs, then running back to the people and barking wildly.

"Didn't we have *four* dogs?" Mrs. Newton said.

"Yes," replied Emily.

"Then where are the other three?" Mrs. Newton asked.

"Finally!" Dolly bowwowed. "They're stuck. I'll

show you where. Follow me now!" She scuttled down the steps and into the interior of the boat.

"I think we better see what she wants us to do," said Ryce.

"George," said Mrs. Newton. "We might need some help here."

"I'm busy driving the boat," said Mr. Newton. "If it's an emergency, let me know."

Ted, Ryce, Emily, and Mrs. Newton followed Dolly down the steps and into the cabins.

Dolly had stopped in front of the low bed and was barking furiously at Chubby's hairy rump.

"They're here!" Dolly yapped wildly. "Help is here, Chubby. You don't have a thing to worry about."

"Mom!" said Emily. "Look! Chubby is stuck. I'll bet the other puppies are stuck under the bed, too!"

Ted knelt down next to Chubby and gently eased her from her tight spot. "There you go!" he said.

Chubby was delighted at finally being set free. She barked happily and licked Ted's face. "Thank you! Thank you!"

Now all of the people were down on their knees looking under the bed. "No more puppies under here," said Ryce.

"But there's that hole back there," said Mrs. Newton. "Do you think they could have crawled down there?"

"That would be just like Moe and Tchaikovsky," said Emily. She knew the puppies best. "They love to explore."

76

"Then I guess they're down there," said Mrs. Newton.

Ted shimmied under the bed as far as he could and tried to shout down the dark hole. "Hey! Moe! Tchaikovsky! Are you down there? Can you hear me, puppies!"

But the only sound any of them could hear was the growling of the twin diesel engines.

"We better go get Daddy," said Ryce.

Emily looked as if she was about to cry. "Oh Mommy! What'll we do? What if Moe and Tchaikovsky are hurt?"

"Don't worry, honey," Mrs. Newton soothed. "Everything will be just fine. Daddy can fix anything." Silently she added: *I hope.*

The moment Mr. Newton saw his family coming up from the cabin he knew something serious had happened—everyone looked worried. Even Dolly and Chubby seemed subdued.

"You found one of them, I see," he shouted over the rumbling of the big engines. "Where are the others?"

"We think that they're trapped somewhere in the boat. It could be underneath the deck," said Mrs. Newton.

"That's ''tween decks,'" Mr. Newton corrected nautically.

"Whatever," said Mrs. Newton.

"Please rescue them, Daddy," Emily pleaded.

Now, it happened that Mr. Newton had been

itching for a good reason to sneak around down in the engine room, to poke through all the nooks and crannies in the guts of the boat, but he had been unable to think of one—short of actual engine trouble, and he did not want that.

"Well," he said, "let's see what we can do about this. . . ." He pulled back on the throttle and shut down the engine. Suddenly there was nothing but silence in the air; the only sounds were the blowing of the wind and the lapping of the waves against the hull of the ship.

But then they heard something else. . . . Muffled and vague, as if it was coming from very far away, the Newtons could hear the howls of two very scared, panicky puppies.

Emily immediately put her ear to the deck. "They're down there!" she exclaimed. "I can hear them better."

Dolly and Chubby heard the passionate yowling of their brothers, too, and they took up the cry, howling at the top of their lungs.

Mr. Newton opened a big hatch in the deck of the boat, exposing the innards of the ship to the light of day. It was a deep dark hole crammed with machinery, fuel tanks, and electrical wiring. It smelled of oil and gas, and the engines threw off a lot of heat. As soon as the hatch went up, though, they all could hear the puppies much, much louder.

"They're down there!" said Emily. "I told you they were down there. Daddy, go and get them!"

"Now nobody touch anything," Mr. Newton cautioned as he took a flashlight from the toolbox. "I'm going down there right now."

Very carefully, he lowered himself into the cramped space, bending over to fit himself under the deck. He managed to crawl forward a few feet, then—*wham!*—cracked his forehead on a low beam.

"Ow! Ouch! Darn!" The sudden blinding pain made him want to stand upright, and as he did so he banged the top of his head against the underside of the deck.

"Yeow!" Mr. Newton felt himself falling over, so he put a hand out to steady himself, groping blindly—and then he touched the hot engine!

"YEEEEEEEEEEOOOOOOOOWWWWWW!" he said, as well a number of other things that cannot be repeated here.

Moe and Tchaikovsky thought he was yowling at them, so they howled back even louder. Dolly and Chubby heard all that howling and just couldn't help themselves—they just *had* to join in!

"Daddy?" asked Emily. "What are you doing down there?"

"I just banged my head twice!" Mr. Newton shouted angrily. "And I burned my hand on the engine!"

"George! Are you all right?" said Mrs. Newton, her voice full of worry.

"Yes, yes," grumbled Mr. Newton.

"How about the puppies?" asked Emily. "Are they all right, too?"

"How should I know? I haven't found them yet."

"Well, keep looking, Daddy."

Muttering under his breath about the unfairness of life, Mr. Newton crept forward a few more feet.

He shone the flashlight ahead of him, but still could not see Tchaikovsky and Moe. To his immense disappointment, Mr. Newton was finding that exploring the inside of the boat was not nearly as much fun as he had hoped it would be. A few minutes ago he had been up on the bridge of this beautiful boat, sailing through clear blue water, happy as a bird in a breeze. Now he was bent over double, his head hurt in two places, his hand was burned, and he was sweating profusely. It was hot down there!

He wiped his hand across his forehead to clear off the perspiration that had built up there. (He would not find out till a little later that he had left a big, black, oily smear in its place.)

"Daddy?" called Emily.

"I'm working on it, Emily, okay," Mr. Newton muttered between tightly clenched teeth.

George had crawled all the way forward to the wall that separated the engine room from the cabins. He knelt down and directed the beam of the flashlight along the base of the wall. And there, sticking out of one of the ventilation ducts, was the little round head of Moe.

"We're saved!" Moe yelped.

Mr. Newton squirmed forward on his stomach and grasped Moe firmly by the scruff of the neck

80

and yanked him out of the pipe like a cork out of a bottle. No sooner was Moe out than Tchaikovsky's head popped up where Moe's had been.

"Me, too!" squealed Tchaikovsky. "Don't forget me!"

"Calm down," said Mr. Newton. "Calm down." He pulled Tchaikovsky from the ventilation shaft, tucked both puppies under his arm like furry footballs, and carefully made his way back to the opening on the deck.

Ted, Ryce, Emily, and Mrs. Newton clapped and cheered when George emerged from the dark interior of the boat. Dolly and Chubby jumped up and down and barked in delight when they saw that Moe and Tchaikovsky were safe and sound.

Emily grabbed the puppies and hugged them tight. "Don't ever do that again!" she said sternly. "That was very naughty of you, you know. You have to be more careful about what you do on the boat. You could have been hurt."

Alice embraced George warmly. "My hero," she said, laughing.

"My dear," Mr. Newton replied, "I must return to my post. I am the commander of this vessel."

"Aye, aye, sir!"

12
•••

The *Day by Day* sailed into the little harbor at
Sutton's Bay just as the sun was beginning to
set. There were very few boats in the marina, the
water was calm, and practically no wind was blowing, so Mr. Newton didn't have too much trouble
guiding his boat into its place at the dock. Ted,
Ryce, and Mrs. Newton worked their lines just
right, while Emily gathered up the puppies and
kept them from getting in the way or under everyone's feet.

Mr. Newton shut down the engine and beamed at
his family. "Well, crew," he said proudly, "our first
voyage is completed without a hitch."

"What's he so happy about?" Tchaikovsky grumbled. "I had a lousy time stuck down there in that pipe."

But Moe, adventurous as always, was a little more easygoing. The frightening experience of getting stuck down below was already beginning to fade from his memory—he was ready for some new adventures.

"This is supposed to be a very pretty town," said Mrs. Newton. "Let's go take a look around."

That was just what Moe wanted to hear. "Terrific! Let's go!" he yelped, and jumped for the side of the boat.

"Kids! Remember we have an agreement!" said Mr. Newton. "You have to keep the puppies under control."

"I'll get the leashes," said Ryce, going below.

"Awwww," said Moe. "Leashes? That's no fun. . . ."

The family strolled the streets of Sutton's Bay—or rather George and Alice Newton strolled while the kids got yanked along by the puppies, who were anxious to see and smell everything the little town had to offer. There was nothing that didn't interest the little dogs, so they would surge along the sidewalk and then suddenly come to a screeching halt when they noticed a particular point of interest or picked up a new scent.

"Both my arms are getting yanked out of their sockets!" complained Ted. He had Moe and Tchaikovsky on leashes.

"I don't think they like the leashes very much," said Emily.

Suddenly all the dogs stopped and sniffed the air, their noses trembling. "I smell birds," said Chubby.

"Me, too," said Tchaikovsky.

"Big, big birds!" said Dolly, her bark full of excitement.

They turned the corner and came to the village green, a small park in the middle of the town, with a large duck pond in the center. On the pond, swimming around, quacking, minding their own business, were some ducks.

"Yowza!" said Moe. "Big ducks!" And he was off! He took Ted completely by surprise, yanking the leash out of the boy's hand and racing straight for the hapless ducks in the pond.

The other three puppies saw what Moe had done and joined in the chase, tearing away from the Newtons as fast as their legs would carry them. Moe, followed closely by Tchaikovsky, Chubby and Dolly, hit the pond, splashing into the water and barking at the tops of their voices.

"Oh no!" shouted Mr. Newton. "Come on! Get back here!"

Ted, Emily, and Ryce were chasing after the dogs, shouting and waving their arms madly, desperately trying to get the dogs to pay attention to them.

But the puppies were having too much fun to pay them any mind at all. They were charging through the shallow water of the pond, diving for the ducks, barking and howling.

85

The ducks had no idea what was going on. One moment they were swimming around their pond nibbling on bits of bread that passersby had tossed in the water for them—the next moment they were being chased by a horde of canine maniacs. And those humans making all that commotion on the banks of the pond weren't helping things at all!

The puppies were splashing happily and barking, running at the ducks every time one settled on the water. The ducks looked like they were getting sick of this game, so when it became apparent that the little dogs were not going to give them a moment of peace, they simply flapped their wings and flew away. They honked and quacked indignantly as they did so.

The puppies stopped, ankle-deep in the water, and watched the unhappy ducks' getaway.

"Awwwww," said Chubby. "Where are you going?"

"The game was just getting started," griped Dolly.

"Birds are no fun at all," said Moe.

"They're almost as boring and weird as humans," said Tchaikovsky.

"Speaking of humans . . . Where are the Newtons?" Chubby asked.

Right at that moment all the Newtons except Alice sploshed into the pond, trying to grab the four leashes.

"Hold it right there, puppies!" Mr. Newton ordered. He reached to snatch Moe's leash, lost his

86

footing in the muddy bottom of the pond, and toppled—*kerplosh!*—into the murky water.

"Who said humans are boring?" Moe yapped. "Look! Mr. Newton has come to play with us!"

All of a sudden all of the dogs and the kids were running around in the water. It was like a wild game of tag, with the humans chasing the dogs and the dogs staying just out of reach.

"Come on!" Ryce shouted. "Stop it!"

"Heel! Heel!" George Newton yelled. "Stop!"

Emily knew that the puppies were having fun— but she also knew that they would pay for it. Mr. Newton would not be happy about this at all. She stood at the water's edge pleading with the puppies to behave.

"Please, please, *please* . . . Puppies, Daddy's going to be so mad . . . please come out of the water."

Finally, Ted made a dive for Dolly and got hold of her leash—but he went headfirst into the water in the process. Dolly was so excited by the game that the little puppy dragged the boy a few feet as if he were a water-skier.

Seeing that Ted had more or less succeeded in capturing a puppy, Ryce and Mr. Newton tried the same thing. They fell on the puppies, grabbed their leashes, and yanked them out of the water, pulling them up on the grass bank.

All the puppies, as well as Ted, Ryce, and Mr. Newton, were dripping wet and covered with mud. The humans were panting from the struggle to recapture their dogs, but Moe, Tchaikovsky, Chubby, and Dolly thought that the game was still going on. They jumped and frisked and barked, trying to get the game started again.

"Okay! Okay!" Moe yapped. "You won the first round! Good going! Now let's start the second half!"

"Down, Moe, down!" said Ryce.

"Bad puppies," said Ted, doing his best to sound really angry. "Baaaaaad, baaaad puppies."

"I'm telling you!" Mr. Newton shouted angrily. "These puppies are ruining this whole trip!"

"Now, George, it's not so bad. . . ."

Mr. Newton rolled his eyes and shook his head. "I get in a bullfight! I sleep in the car! I bang my head! Burn my hand! Now I'm soaking wet! This is the last time I am ever going to try—"

He stopped in the middle of his angry speech when he noticed that the antics of the dogs and the Newtons had attracted a fairly large crowd. All of a sudden it looked as if the entire community had come out to watch the mischief-making of the Newtons and their pets.

Mr. Newton looked around at the people, feeling like a fool. In fact the entire family felt ridiculous.

"Hi!" said Mr. Newton with a big, phony smile.

Mrs. Newton waved.

Ryce closed her eyes and wished that the ground would open at her feet and swallow her up. "I am so embarrassed," she whispered. "Daddy, make them go away. Puh-leeze!"

"Okay," said Mr. Newton, stepping forward and

88

addressing the crowd. "Sorry about all that. Our dogs got loose and . . . uh, they're just, uh, puppies, and they thought we were playing with them, but . . . Anyway, okay. So that's it. Sorry."

Mr. Newton slunk back to his family. "I feel like such an idiot."

Then a very commanding voice called out: "Okay, folks, break it up, the show is over. . . ." A policeman stepped out of the crowd and walked across the lawn toward the Newtons.

"Uh-oh," said Mr. Newton.

"Evening, folks," said the policeman. "How are you all doing tonight?"

All the Newtons smiled sick little smiles. "Fine," they all said.

"That's good. I'm guessing you're not from around here, are you?"

"Right," said Mr. Newton.

The policeman took his ticket book from his back pocket. "Would you care to tell me what was going on here?"

"Well, we were out for a walk," said Mr. Newton, "taking in the sights here in your beautiful, beautiful little town. Alice, kids, don't we think this is just a beautiful little place?"

"Oh, yes," said Ryce.

"Enchanting," said Mrs. Newton.

"So," Mr. Newton continued. "We were out taking a walk, spending our tourist dollars in local businesses and enterprises, when our little dogs here got away from us and started chasing the ducks in

your absolutely charming little duck pond there."
George did his best to force a laugh.

"And you know how puppies are, they got a little overexcited and they wouldn't answer our commands . . . I admit it, things got a little out of hand. . . ."

"But no harm done," said Mrs. Newton.

The policeman had scarcely moved a muscle during this lengthy explanation. "Uh-huh . . . Let me see, how many pups do you have here? Four?" He flipped open his ticket book. "That's four untethered animals, plus a twenty-five-dollar fine—"

"I don't believe it! You're giving me a ticket?"

"Nope," said the policeman.

"Thank goodness!" said Mrs. Newton.

"I'm giving you three tickets."

"Three!"

"One ticket for having untethered animals, one ticket for disturbing the peace, and one ticket for frightening the ducks."

"Frightening the ducks! You can't do this!"

"Can you give me one good reason why I can't?"

"Because—"

"Waaaaaaah!" Emily cried loudly.

"Oh honey," said Alice, kneeling down next to her, "there's nothing to cry about." She glanced at the policeman. "Well, not much, anyway."

But Emily refused to allow herself to be consoled by her mother. Her words came out in a passionate rush. "The policeman is going to give Daddy a ticket, and because he's getting a ticket, Daddy's going to get rid of Moe and Tchaikovsky and Chubby and Dolly!"

The dogs heard their names and saw that Emily was crying. They knew that could not be a good thing. The puppies began to whine and whimper and looked very, very unhappy.

"I want my doggies!" Emily wailed. Then she threw her arms around the policeman's leg. "Pleeeeeeze, Mister Policeman! Please don't let them take away my puppies!"

"Harooooo!" the puppies wailed.

The policeman turned to Mr. Newton. "You . . . you wouldn't take away this little girl's puppies, would you?"

Mr. Newton shook his head slowly. "Well . . . it's hard to say. Emily and I *did* have an understanding and this little incident in the duck pond does suggest that our understanding isn't working out."

"Daddy! Please! They'll be good," Emily sobbed. "I promise they'll be good. I'll make sure they're good."

"But, Emily, if I have to worry about paying tickets every time the puppies make a nuisance of themselves . . ."

The policeman was acutely embarrassed by the whole scene. He hated to hear the little girl crying so miserably.

"Look," he said quickly, "I have a little girl of my own. I know how kids can be, so if I forget about the tickets, will you let your little daughter keep her little puppies?"

"Well . . ." said Mr. Newton, "I don't know about that."

"Please, Daddy."

"Come on, mister," the cop pleaded. "Have a heart. Listen to her. It's breaking her heart."

"Oh . . . okay."

"That's great!" The policeman tore up the sheaf of tickets and tossed them in a nearby trash can. "Well, I guess I've kept you good people too long as it is. Enjoy your stay in Sutton's Bay."

He tried to walk away, but Emily still clung to his leg. "Ah, little girl? You can let go of my leg now."

"Oh," said Emily brightly, "sorry." She unclasped the policeman's leg and smiled sweetly at him. "Thank you. Bye-bye."

"Right, so long."

Emily's tears were gone and she was as amiable and as pleasant as she usually was. The change was astonishing—it was as if the sun had come out from behind a cloud and dried her cheeks.

"Whew," said Mr. Newton as he watched the policeman walk back to his police cruiser. "That was close."

"But you didn't get a ticket, Dad," said Ted.

"Yes, I know. Thank goodness for that!"

"It was all because of Emily," said Ryce. "Good going, Emily. You saved Dad a lot of money."

Mrs. Newton looked down at her youngest child, her eyes narrowed as if she was trying to look into

Emily's mind. "Emily?" she asked. "Were those tears of yours really genuine?"

Emily fluttered her eyelashes and looked sweetly at her mother. "I'll never tell," she said.

13

•••

There was no way that Mr. Newton was going to let four dirty puppies set foot on his immaculate boat. As the family made their way back to the marina, they passed through the boatyard and Mr. Newton had a very bright idea.

"Keep the puppies here," he told his children. "I'll be back in a minute."

"What's this all about?" Moe asked no one in particular.

"More human weirdness," Dolly answered.

Then things got *really* weird!

Without a word of warning, a spurt of water

came out of nowhere and hit Tchaikovsky in the chest.

"Hey!" the little dog shrieked, so surprised he almost jumped out of his skin. "Cut it out!"

It was Mr. Newton with the boatyard hose and he was busy spraying water at the dogs. The dogs were scurrying around dodging and jumping to get away from the spray of water.

"Revenge is sweet!" Mr. Newton hollered. "Now this—*this* is fun." He continued to spray the dogs, cackling to himself as they ran around in crazy circles trying to avoid getting clean.

After showering the dogs at random, Mr. Newton began to concentrate on them one by one. First he sprayed Chubby until she was completely soaked and clean.

"Okay, as I get them clean, take them back to the boat."

"Right, Dad," said Ryce. She snatched up Chubby and ran with her, making for the boat. "We have to get you dry, little girl."

It was Tchaikovsky's turn next. The relentless stream of water pinned him in a corner of the yard and in a matter of seconds he was drenched to the skin.

"Grab him, Ted!"

Ted picked up Tchaikovsky, tucked him in the crook of the arm like a football, and raced toward the boat like a running back.

Emily got hold of a completely soaked Dolly. "Come on, Dolly, let's go dry off."

Mr. Newton handled Moe. As he carried the puppy back to the boat, the little dog asked a question.

"Now what on earth was that all about?"

Now the Newtons themselves had to get cleaned up. It's not easy to take a shower on a boat. The shower stalls are small and the amount of water that comes out of the shower head is not as great as in a normal bathroom on dry land.

And there was one other thing. . . . By the time Ted, Ryce, and Emily had gotten cleaned up and it was Mr. Newton's turn to take a shower, there was no hot water left in the boat's water tanks.

Mr. Newton folded himself into the tiny shower stall, turned on the water, and grumbled loudly when the cold water hit his skin. The lack of space and the cold water made the shower very unpleasant, but it was particularly difficult to take a shower when you were trying to get wet and at the same time trying to avoid getting any cold water on you.

He soaped himself up as best as he could and put shampoo in his hair and was trying to get the whole bothersome process over and done with when the water gave out completely!

"Huh? What's going on?"

His eyes were closed tight against the soap on his head, so he couldn't see a thing. Groping blindly, he got hold of the handle to the shower stall and tried to push it open. But it wouldn't budge.

"Now what!" he said angrily. He jiggled the door handle and pushed and pushed, but he couldn't get the door open. Then he started rapping on the glass.

"Alice! Alice!" he shouted. "Come and get me out of here!"

Up on deck, Mrs. Newton was setting the folding table so the family could have dinner outside. Ryce was drying her hair and the loud noise made it almost impossible to hear anything in the interior of the boat.

"Daddy's taking a long time," she remarked.

"Maybe he was really dirty," said Emily.

The puppies, on the other hand, had much better hearing than any human. They could hear Mr. Newton pounding and hollering.

"Hey!" said Moe. "Hear that?"

"Yup," said Tchaikovsky.

"Let's go take a look."

"Oh, no," said Dolly. "No more exploring for you two."

"I'm not going exploring," said Moe defensively. "I'm just going to see what all the commotion is about, that's all."

"Me, too," said Tchaikovsky.

"Then I'm coming along to make sure you two don't get yourself in a jam again," said Dolly.

Chubby, who hated to be left out of anything, popped up at this moment. "I guess I'll come along, too."

The four little dogs strolled down into the boat and sat outside the bathroom listening to Mr. Newton's irate shouts and insistent pounding on the wall.

"Alice! Alice! Anybody!" he bellowed. "Would someone come down here and get me out of this thing?"

The four puppies were seated there on the floor like people at a theater watching a play.

"Wow," said Chubby. "He is really mad, isn't he?"

"Yup, but I heard him madder than that."

"Right." Dolly nodded. "Like the time the leg got chewed off the chair in the den, remember?"

"Oh yes," said Tchaikovsky. "I remember. That's about the most mad I've ever seen him."

"Oh, that was nothing," said Moe. "What about the time all four of us chewed up every one of his socks?"

"Oh, right," said Chubby. "I forgot about that time."

Mr. Newton had stopped rattling and shouting. He was silent for a moment, then he started thumping against the door with his shoulder, using all his strength to batter his way through the tin partition.

"Have you ever seen Dad open a door?" asked Moe.

"Yes," said Tchaikovsky. "He just hops up on his hind legs and pushes it with his front paws."

"Then why can't Mr. Newton do it?" asked Chubby.

"Oh, come on," said Moe. "The answer is obvious. Dad is a hundred times smarter than Mr. Newton!"

"Really!" Dolly agreed.

"I think I'll give it a try," said Moe. He stood on his hind legs and fell with a thump against the door. It didn't budge.

"Let's all try," said Tchaikovsky.

"Okay," said Moe. "All together!"

Eight puppy paws hit the door and pushed it open.

"What the—!" Mr. Newton came tumbling out and toppled to the floor, sliding a few feet because his skin was slick with soap.

"Hi," barked Moe.

Slightly dazed, Mr. Newton looked at the door. It opened in and he had been pushing out!

It was a lovely moonlit night, quiet and cool. The family had finished dinner and it was time for bed.

Mr. Newton went below and folded down the three beds—it was like a triple-decker bunk bed— that the children would use.

"Now, you'll be in here," Mrs. Newton explained as she tucked the children in. "And Daddy and I will be in the cabin in the bow."

A few minutes later the lights were out. Everyone was in bed and falling asleep to the gentle lilt of the boat rocking on the calm waters.

In the middle of the night all that changed. The storm came without warning. First there was a light sprinkling of rain—*then* came a blinding white flash of lightning and then the roar of a thunderclap as loud as an explosion!

100

Everyone awoke at the same time. Emily started crying, the puppies started howling, and the boat started rocking as the vicious winds whipped up the waters on the lake.

Mr. and Mrs. Newton were out of bed in a split second. Mrs. Newton hurried to calm the children while Mr. Newton went up on deck to make sure that neither the boat nor his family was in any danger.

The water was very choppy and the rain was pouring down in solid sheets. In an instant Mr. Newton was soaked to the skin. The harbor was well protected from the main part of the lake and he was satisfied that there was no immediate danger. He went back inside, reaching for a towel as he went.

All of his children and all of the dogs were gone from the main cabin and were now tucked up in his bed. Everyone jumped every time there was a peal of thunder or a flash of lightning.

"Daddy," asked Emily in a small, scared voice. "Are we okay here? Nothing is going to happen to us, is it?"

"No, honey," said Mr. Newton reassuringly. "There's nothing to worry about at all."

"You sure?"

"Yes, dear. Hey, is there room for me in my own bed?"

"Make room for Daddy," said Alice Newton.

"There isn't any room left, Dad," said Ted.

"May I suggest that you get rid of the dogs?"

"Awwwww," said Tchaikovsky. "No fair!"

Emily, Ryce, and Ted reluctantly relinquished the puppy each was holding like a living stuffed toy.

"Well," said Moe, "I knew that was too good to last!"

The puppies fell in a soft heap at the base of the bed and fell asleep.

14

• • •

The next morning there was hardly a trace of the terrible storm that had struck the night before. The sun was shining bright, the sky was clear and blue—the only sign of the storm was the very stiff breeze that was blowing.

The *Day by Day* set sail just after nine in the morning, the bow bashing through the choppy water. They had been sailing for only twenty-five minutes when Ted got a funny look on his face.

"You know," he said. "I don't feel too good."

Ryce had the same look on her face, too. "Me neither."

"Uh-oh," said Mrs. Newton. "Maybe you better go down to the cabin and lie down."

"Oh, I can't, Mom," said Ryce. "I can't go down there. I need fresh air. But this boat rocking is making me sick."

The puppies had been listening intently. "I know what they mean," said Tchaikovsky. "I'm not feeling so hot myself."

"Me neither," admitted Dolly.

"Or me," said Moe.

"I feel fine," said Chubby. "So if you guys don't feel like eating lunch, get it anyway and I'll take it."

Dolly's eyes almost crossed. "Ugh," she said. "The very thought of food makes me sick."

"Don't talk about it," said Tchaikovsky. "I don't want to hear anything about food, okay?"

Mrs. Newton went up to the cockpit to speak to her husband. "George, I think we have a problem. Ted and Ryce—" She looked at her husband. His skin was sort of green and he was sweating quite a bit.

"Oh, no," said Alice. "Not you, too!"

Sailors always think that they should never, ever get seasick. It's a badge of shame.

"I'm fine!" said Mr. Newton.

"No, you're not! You're as green as a frog! And you're sweating like a pig, too!"

"It's hot," Mr. Newton insisted.

"No, it's not," Mrs. Newton countered. "You're seasick!"

"Uh-uh."

"Well, if you're not seasick, maybe I should go down to the kitchen—"

"Galley," Mr. Newton corrected.

"Galley, kitchen—whatever. I'll go down there and cook up some nice fried eggs with hot Tabasco sauce and some nice greasy sausage. Then I'll get you some raw oysters and a plate of cooked kidneys. I know how you love to eat; remember all those hamburgers you ate that time?"

Mr. Newton didn't look green anymore. He looked gray. "Take the wheel," he gasped.

"Take the wheel?" Alice asked. "Take it where?"

"Drive," he wheezed. "Just drive the boat."

Mrs. Newton settled in the captain's chair and took the wheel in her hands. In front of her were a radar screen, a compass, and a lot of controls she knew nothing about. Well, not quite—there was one that she understood. The one marked HORN.

"I guess I'm okay if I don't run into anything," she said aloud. "Or sink," she added a moment later.

Down below, the remaining Newtons and their dogs were not happy sailors. Only Chubby and Emily seemed immune to the rocking of the boat. Those two didn't feel the slightest bit sick.

"So what's it like?" Emily asked Ted. "Does your head hurt?"

"Ohhhh," Ted groaned.

"Is that a yes?"

"Ohhhhhhhhhh," Ted moaned.

"Are you sick to your stomach?"

105

"Please, Emily," said Ted unhappily.

"Like you're going to throw up?"

Ted staggered to his feet. "I'm going to lie down. If you hear anyone hurling down here, it's me."

"Don't talk about it!" squealed Ryce.

"I'm sorry," said Ted. "I've got to lie down."

"I wish I could," Ryce groaned. "But I won't be able to breathe down there. I know I won't."

This interested Emily greatly. "Really? It's that bad, huh? Tell me what it's like, Ryce."

"Emily, please . . ." Ryce begged. "Emily, please leave me alone. Leave me to die in peace."

Just then, Mr. Newton stumbled down from the wheelhouse. Emily gaped at him with wide eyes.

"Daddy! If you're down here, who's driving the boat?"

"Mommy," gasped Mr. Newton.

"Wow!" said Emily. "This I've got to see! Come on, Chubby." The little girl and her little dog climbed to the upper deck.

Mrs. Newton was more relaxed now. She was sitting there, holding the wheel, watching the horizon and humming to herself.

"Mommy!" Emily exclaimed. "You're the captain now! Everybody downstairs is sick! Even Moe, Tchaikovsky, and Dolly!"

"What are we going to do about this, Emily?" Mrs. Newton asked. "We can't go on like this indefinitely."

Emily nodded vigorously. "I know. People down there are going to start hurling pretty soon."

"Hurling! Where did you learn that word?"

"From Ted."

"Well," said Mrs. Newton, "tell him not to do that anymore. . . . You know, we have to get back on dry land and in a hurry!"

"Yes," Emily replied. "I think we do, too."

Chubby was sprawled on her back, enjoying the feeling of the warm sun on her belly. "Oh, I don't know," she said. "It's pretty good out here. I'm a little on the hungry side, but other than that . . ."

"But where do we go?" asked Emily.

Mrs. Newton looked around. They were out of sight of land and there was nothing to see but deep blue water. Suddenly she felt a little nervous. This was more of a predicament than she had bargained for.

Alice leaned forward and peered at the radar screen. She could see that there was a course plotted on it, a line stretching from Sutton's Bay to Silver Birch Island. There was a small blinking dot on the screen. "That must be us," she said. "Daddy had it all worked out. All we have to do is stay on this line and we'll be okay. At least, I think that's how it is supposed to work."

"Wow," said Emily. "Dad did all that?"

"Yes, he did."

"Gee, I guess it's a shame that he doesn't have the stomach to be a sailor."

Mrs. Newton giggled. "Yes, but don't tell him that."

Gradually, as the boat sailed on, the low outline of Silver Birch Island appeared on the horizon. Mrs. Newton turned the wheel on course, coming around the southern end of the island and under the protection of a spit of land that thrust out into the lake. The waves died down immediately, and as they did so, Ted, Ryce, and Mr. Newton—along with Tchaikovsky, Moe, and Dolly—began to feel better.

Mr. Newton came back up on the bridge. He looked pale and wan, but definitely on the mend.

"I'll take over now," he said to his wife.

"No fair," said Mrs. Newton. "I do all the work and you get all the glory!"

"I don't think you're ready to put the boat in a berth," said Mr. Newton.

"I hope you know what you're doing, George," said Mrs. Newton, handing over the wheel.

"Just get hold of your line, honey," said Mr. Newton. "I'll take care of everything else."

The three still-sick puppies swarmed onto the deck and gazed at the island from the rail of the boat.

"Real dry land!" Moe howled. "I've never been so happy to see land in my entire life!"

"Me, too!" said Dolly.

"Me three!" said Tchaikovsky.

"Oh, I don't know," said Chubby. "We had a pretty good time up there. Me and Mrs. Newton and Emily. I'm sorry you missed it. . . ."

"One day you'll get sick," said Dolly. "And I won't feel sorry for you one little bit!"

Mr. Newton still did not feel a hundred percent well. Perhaps that was why he came in toward the dock a little too fast. The speed made him bump the dock a little too hard.

And it was a bump that shook the boat from bow to stern!

The next thing Mr. Newton heard was a loud cry from the stern of the boat.

"Puppies overboard!"

15
...

The four little dogs plunged into the water head-first. They disappeared beneath the surface for a second or two, then four furry heads burst back up, the puppies yapping and yelping.

"Wow!" shouted Moe. "What happened!"

"We fell in the water!" yapped Tchaikovsky.

"I know that!"

The puppies didn't really mind being in the water—after all, the doggy paddle came naturally to them—but the entire Newton family was completely freaked out!

"Daddy! Mommy!" Emily shrieked. "The puppies fell in the water! Save them!"

"I'll get them!" said Ted, and jumped into the water with all his clothes on.

"Ted!" shouted Ryce. "Don't!" She jumped in after him.

"Oh no!" Mr. Newton yelled. There was nothing else he could do. He jumped into the water, too.

"Look at that," said Chubby. "Ted, Ryce, and Mr. Newton have come in swimming with us!"

The puppies swam around for a few moments then climbed out of the water and stood on the dock watching Ted, Ryce, and Mr. Newton floundering around, splashing in the water.

"Well," said Moe, "that's kind of interesting. But I want to look around now that I'm back on dry land." He shook the water out of his thick coat then ran down the dock.

"Wait for me!" howled Tchaikovsky.

"Oh, no," said Dolly. "Here we go again!"

The Newtons decided that if the puppies wanted to go exploring, then the whole family would go exploring, too. After Mr. Newton hauled himself out of the water and dried himself off, he went to the marina store and rented five bicycles. They put a puppy in each of the four bushel baskets—Mrs. Newton didn't get one—and pedaled up the main street of Silver Birch Island.

This was a totally new sensation for the puppies and each of them sat up straight in their basket, tongue out, ears flapping, enjoying the rushing of

112

the wind as the Newton family pedaled along as fast as they could.

Once they got to town, Mrs. Newton bought the makings of a picnic lunch and then they rode out of town, pushing the bikes up a steep hill, at the top of which they stopped and unpacked their food.

It was a beautiful spot on the side of the road, and as they ate their sandwiches they could see the lake spread before them and could look down on the town and the marina. From far away like this, their big boat looked like a bathtub toy.

"This is so nice," said Ryce, her morning bout with seasickness forgotten.

"Sure is," Ted agreed.

The puppies romped and gamboled in the tall grass, stopping every few minutes to pester the Newtons for treats from their lunch.

Soon it was time for the puppies to get back in their baskets on the bikes. They loved the fast trip back down the hill, the wind whistling through their fur. The puppies really loved to go fast!

When the family returned to the boat, everyone sort of drifted away on their own. Ted and Ryce sprawled on the deck with books, Emily played with some toys she had brought along, Mrs. Newton dozed in the cabin, and Mr. Newton went to tidy things up on the bridge.

All of the puppies—except Moe, of course—lazed around in the sun, not doing much. Moe, on the other hand, had detected a fascinating smell on the

113

breeze. He clambered up to the rail of the boat and peered over the side.

Sure enough, he saw what he thought he had smelled. At the far end of the marina were . . . ducks! They were bigger than the ducks in Sutton's Bay, and instead of being brown, these were white. And they didn't quack, they honked like old-fashioned car horns!

They were swimming along, going from boat to boat, hoping that someone would toss them a cookie or a scrap of bread. Moe hunched down on the deck, trying to make himself as small as possible, lying in wait for the unsuspecting big white ducks.

As the birds sailed closer, Moe felt the excitement build inside of him. At exactly the right moment he was going to jump up and give those ducks the scare of their life!

A second later Moe was ready to pounce. The ducks were right next to the boat now, four or five of them. The little dog suddenly jumped to his feet and started barking furiously—*bowwowow-wowow!* The ducks were taken by surprise and flapped their big wings for a moment, but they didn't run away.

They stared at the little dog for a split second or two, then they got really angry. They honked loudly then flew right up onto the deck of the boat.

"You rotten little dog!" one of them honked.

"Think you could scare us!" said another.

114

The birds hissed and honked and nipped at Moe's nose with their long bills.

"Yeow!" screamed Moe. "That hurts!"

Suddenly everybody was shouting or yelping or honking!

The ducks closed in on Moe, nipping and snapping at him. His courage drained away and he started to run. Skittering along the deck and across the gangplank, Moe raced away from the birds as fast as he could go. The ducks followed him up onto land, chasing him until he thought he would die from fright!

Finally the ducks decided he had learned his lesson and they returned to the water, swimming away in a snit. His head down with shame, Moe slunk back to the boat.

"Well," said Dolly, "I hope you've learned your lesson now, Mister Moe!"

"Ducks don't usually fight like that," said Moe.

Emily picked him up and squeezed him hard. "Moe, Moe, Moe, are you sure you're all right?"

16
•••

The Newtons sailed around the lake for the next few days, but because of the possibility of seasickness, Mr. Newton was careful never to venture out unless the water was as smooth as glass.

The last night of the cruise, they pulled into the town of Charlevoix and the Newtons decided that they would go into town and have a dinner of celebration. Mr. Newton made one request.

"Please," he begged. "Emily, no dogs . . ."

"Okay, Daddy," said Emily. "I guess you've been a pretty good sport about having the puppies come along."

They shut the puppies up in the cabin with big

bowls of food so they could have their own little celebration.

When the Newtons returned from dinner, they discovered that the puppies not only had eaten their dinner, but they had taken turns chewing on Mr. Newton's captain's hat. They had obviously had a merry time tearing it to shreds.

Mr. Newton picked up the remnants of the hat and looked at it sadly. "Well," he said, "I guess that's the end of the trip. . . ."

"Don't worry, honey," said Mrs. Newton, "you can always get yourself another hat."

"Well . . ." said Mr. Newton, "I was thinking of getting a new hat anyway."

"That's good, dear. You do that."

". . . A new hat to go with the boat I'm going to buy!"